The Ghost and the Writer

"My God!" the soldier exclaimed. "Did you see that?"

John Darnell whirled about and looked in the direction in which the soldier was pointing. Nothing there except a bit of odd haze, but the stairwell door swung gently back in place, and stopped.

The soldier hobbled over to Darnell. "It was a ghost, if you ask me," he said. "First it was there; then there was a puff of smoke and it disappeared."

"Dammit! I missed him." Darnell ran down the corridor to the stairwell and burst through the doorway, looking down the stairs. Nothing. He returned to the corridor.

"Your ghost is gone." He rubbed his forehead. "What did he look like? Can you describe him?"

The soldier, Ernest Hemingway, nodded. "I've seen the insides of more than a couple hospitals, and I've seen the faces of men there, walking ghosts of men, some not in their own minds anymore. But his face—his face—" He shuddered. "Like a ghost, as I said. Pasty white. A very white ghostly face."

Also by Sam McCarver

THE CASE
OF THE UNINVITED
GUEST

A JOHN DARNELL MYSTERY

Sam McCarver

A SIGNET BOOK

SIGNET
Published by New American Library, a division of
Penguin Putnam Inc., 375 Hudson Street,
New York, New York 10014, U.S.A.
Penguin Books Ltd, 80 Strand,
London WC2R 0RL, England
Penguin Books Australia Ltd, Ringwood,
Victoria, Australia
Penguin Books Canada Ltd, 10 Alcorn Avenue,
Toronto, Ontario, Canada M4V 3B2
Penguin Books (N.Z.) Ltd, 182–190 Wairau Road,
Auckland 10, New Zealand

Penguin Books Ltd, Registered Offices:
Harmondsworth, Middlesex, England

First published by Signet, an imprint of New American Library,
a division of Penguin Putnam Inc.

First Printing, August 2002
10 9 8 7 6 5 4 3 2 1

 REGISTERED TRADEMARK—MARCA REGISTRADA

Printed in the United States of America

For my daughter Stacee—
who has a special affinity for Paris

AUTHOR'S NOTE

During World War I, France endured many bloody battles on its soil. Entire armies holed up in trenches, stalemated, for months on end. Seventy miles from Paris, the huge German cannon "Big Bertha" hurled shells that exploded, devastatingly and randomly, through the city. Armistice Day, November 11, 1918, brought enormous relief and a desire to forget the war.

As triumphant allied troops marched in Paris, people celebrated at parties in luxury hotels. But in this novel, a murder during a party at Le Grand Hotel triggers a haunting by a ghostly figure and an investigation of those sightings by Professor John Darnell, the world's first and only paranormal detective. Darnell achieved worldwide prominence solving the *Titanic*'s cabin 13 jinx in 1912, investigating a woman's apparition on the Orient Express in 1914 and the disappearance at a London séance in 1916 of the Prime Minister's daughter, and finding a serial killer whose crimes in 1917 hauntingly resembled those of Jack the Ripper.

In *The Case of The Uninvited Guest*, a youthful Ernest Hemingway, then a wounded soldier, and the young silent film star Mary Miles Minter are enmeshed in this mystery and enthralled by romance in Paris. Most of it derives from my imagination, this "history-mystery" being a work of fiction, in which my characters become real people and real people become my characters.

This book owes its intriguing cover to NAL's brilliant design artists, its editing to my perceptive editor, Genny Ostertag, and its manuscript reviews to NAL's eagle-eyed copyediting staff—all of whom I thank. I thank my literary agent, Donald Maass, for his encouragement and guidance. And for their continued support, I thank my readers—as do, I might say, John and Penny Darnell.

Prologue

Two million jubilant souls cheered President Woodrow Wilson in his proud victory parade through the streets of Paris in mid-December 1918, celebrating the end on November 11 of the war that left poppy fields red with blood and took over ten million lives.

On December 17, in Martin Prince's Royal Suite 999 of Le Grand Hotel, one of the many celebratory parties held that week in the "City of Light" continued noisily with talk and music late into the evening. But Prince, host of the party and Editorial Director of American-Universal Publishing Company, glared about the room, drank heavily, and nursed his feelings of depression. His trip to Paris to meet with writers, publishers, booksellers, businessmen, and others in the book world had even attracted one of Hollywood's most popular actresses to his entourage—but still had utterly failed. He felt the writers had let him down. Yet he knew his company's management would blame only him.

He watched the actress in the group—Mary Miles Minter, a young beauty of only sixteen already with twenty-six silent movies to her credit—as she deftly

fended off the advances of English multimillionaire
David Fitch. Mary's mother, Charlotte Shelby, showing what some would see as natural jealousy of trying to compete with a much younger and more
beautiful daughter, silently fumed. Prince saw that
his associate, Patricia August, also looked on the proceedings with disdain.

Farther across the room, under the glittering chandelier on the other side of the black ebony grand
piano, Eric Thorndyke, a wealthy Hollywood film
writer and producer now living in London but in
Paris for Prince's meetings, was talking spiritedly
with the millionaire Fitch's wife, Cynthia. David
Fitch, in turn, clearly watched them from the corner
of his eye even as he thrust his attentions on the
young actress. Edda Van Eych, seeking publication
of her book and sympathy for her long refuge in
England after fleeing Holland during the war, stood
not far from Thorndyke and Cynthia. Prince doubted
the woman could hear their conversation, although
she seemed to be trying to do so. Ricardo Camilo, a
writer from Spain, who had come to see Martin
Prince about his new book, kept to himself, scowling
bitterly and drinking copious amounts of red wine.
Prince knew Camilo's complaint. He noticed that
when others addressed Camilo, the Spaniard would
respond in his own tongue to put them off.

Brandon Tyler, a true thorn in Prince's side,
seemed to be complaining to anyone who would listen that he might lose his English publishing connection with Prince's American-Universal, based on
hints Prince dropped to him and others about seeking a more aggressive firm. If he lost that business,
Tyler knew his expected luxurious postwar lifestyle

would be jeopardized. For Prince, that was the least of his worries. Tyler had let him down.

Philip Thorndyke was obviously observing the conduct of his father as Eric Thorndyke moved about the room, making advances to every female present after stalking away from Cynthia Fitch. Prince didn't blame the young man. Although Philip had lived in America for five years after his mother's death, Prince knew he'd seen his father on occasion during the war when it was safe to travel. But this trip, after staying with his father in an adjacent suite since their separate arrivals, the son let it be known he was disgusted that the older Thorndyke had become a womanizer.

Prince had encouraged Sylvia Beach, with aspirations of opening a bookstore in Paris, to simply intrude herself quietly into the group. He knew she'd entered into the party with curiosity. She now talked with Bert Ward, an Englishman who seemed to be a general assistant to the Fitches.

During the evening, people came and went from the large suite of rooms, sometimes for private talks, perhaps to return to their own rooms, all conveniently located on the ninth floor, which fit into Prince's plan of having them at his fingertips.

Near midnight, Eric Thorndyke came to Prince, loosening his bow tie. "I—I took too much to drink, Martin. . . . Got to lie down. Can I use your spare bedroom?"

Prince quickly agreed, and Philip Thorndyke helped his father into the bedroom, settling him into a soft chair, as Prince watched. "You'll be all right, then?" Philip asked.

Thorndyke waved a hand. "Just go. I'll sleep it off.

Prince can keep his damn party going as long as he wants. It won't bother me. Close the door."

Philip closed the door and shook his head. "He'll be asleep in minutes," he said, "a drunken sleep."

Some time later, a surreptitious figure opened the secondary hotel corridor door leading into the bedroom and stepped softly inside. In the dim light of the small bed lamp, Thorndyke sprawled, asleep in the chair, red bow tie and cummerbund removed and lying on the table, tuxedo jacket on the bed. *Perfect.* The figure stepped up behind the chair and took out a weapon—a long, slender, tough cord.

With one swift movement, the intruder wrapped the strong cord about the open-collared neck of the sleeping man. Thorndyke gasped and struggled in his drink-induced stupor, tearing at the cord with his hands, his feet thrusting out, his legs twisting.

But the cord, held tightly at each end by the attacker, dug ever more deeply into the man's neck. Blood from the wound spilled down onto Thorndyke's white shirt. His fingers continued to tear desperately at the cord but to no avail. His eyes seemed to protrude from their sockets until he finally stopped jerking and struggling, his face frozen in anguish, arms dropping to his sides, and the life gone from his now-limp body.

The killer stepped over to the corridor door, opened it slightly, turned its locking device, peered out, and left the room.

In the suite's parlor, the piano music, conversation, and hubbub continued, the guests unaware of the death of one of their group on the other side of the bedroom door. But when the party began winding down, not any too soon from Prince's standpoint, Philip Thorndyke stepped back into the bedroom to which his father had retreated and pulled the door closed behind him. Prince checked his watch and hoped the older Thorndyke was over it now and could leave.

But when Philip came out, he looked wild-eyed, distraught, and shouted to the assemblage, "My father's dead! Call the police, someone. Please!" The others crowded about the bedroom door to look, then averted their eyes.

Prince called the *Sûreté* and Jacques Bardon, the Le Grand Hotel manager. Within minutes, Bardon and the hotel doctor, Paul Pascal, rushed up to the suite. Almost an hour later, as Prince rapidly was losing his patience, Inspector Louis Manot of the *Sûreté* arrived and began his investigation, inspecting the scene and interrogating the party guests for several hours.

Had it ended there, with the *Sûreté* investigating the crime competently, Professor John Darnell, the world's first and only paranormal detective, would not have been called in to apply his specialty. But when, a few days later, Jacques Bardon found himself besieged with reports of sightings at midnight of what his hotel guests called, in no uncertain terms, a "ghost," he knew he must seek help.

The first sighting occurred on the Friday night following the Tuesday murder. A couple just checked in for the Christmas holiday saw the apparition in the hall at midnight on the ninth floor, near the Royal

Suite. The woman screamed and threw herself into the arms of her husband. Fifteen minutes later they confronted M'sieur Bardon in his office, the woman in tears, her American husband red-faced and complaining loud enough to be heard outside the office and into the mezzanine lobby.

Bardon took the event seriously and inspected the ninth-floor hall, finding nothing unusual. But the "ninth-floor ghost," as it came to be called, was seen several more nights, until Bardon at last threw up his hands and reached for the telephone.

At the other end of the line, the Chairman of the Board of the hotel, Charles Beauvais, made his points unequivocal. "This must be stopped," he growled into the receiver in French. "And I know the man who can do it." Remembering an account of an apparition aboard the Orient Express before the war, Beauvais telegraphed Professor John Darnell in London, urging that he come to Le Grand to investigate.

Relieved to have taken positive action, Beauvais murmured to himself, *"Mon Dieu!"* and swallowed a stiff jolt of cognac. But he refilled his glass when he realized that with the holidays almost upon them his guests might be frightened by the ghost, even on Christmas Eve and on Christmas. And at midnight on December 24 and December 25, his fears were realized.

Chapter One

The lobby of Le Grand Hotel bustled with clientele checking in and out, heading for dinner at the exclusive mezzanine-level restaurant or for drinks at the bar. Bellmen carried bags to elevators at the far wall or rested them in a holding area for later delivery to rooms. Laughter and excited conversations reverberated throughout the huge domed and vaulted two-story room and up the curved staircase to the mezzanine.

Jacques Bardon, manager of Le Grand Hotel for only one month, had stood nervously behind the hotel's registration desk watching for the arrival of his important guests. He knew René Alain, the head desk clerk standing next to him, considered the great lobby, the bellmen, the clerks to his left and right at the counter, as his little kingdom. But at the moment, Bardon did not stand with ceremony. The murder had changed all that.

Bardon saw approaching, finally, people he knew must be his guests. He bowed from the waist at the six-foot tall, well-dressed man smiling at him across the counter, and gazed into the violet eyes of the auburn-tressed woman holding the man's arm. Tearing his gaze away from her, he said, "Jacques Bardon at your service. It is Professor Darnell, of course, and Mrs. Darnell?"

Darnell nodded. "Thank you for meeting us here. And yes, this is my wife, Penny Darnell."

Bardon smiled through his nervousness. "Just sign your name, Professor, for our clerk, and we'll go on up to my office." To Alain, he said, "Have their bags taken to their room, René."

Alain snapped his fingers and a young bellman hurried to the counter from his station nearby and picked up their bags. Alain gave the bellman a key, and the uniformed man walked away.

Bardon, all smiles, said, "Professor, and madame, follow me, *s'il vous plaît*. We can talk comfortably in my office." He walked to an open-doored elevator, bowed again, motioned to Darnell and Penny to enter, and followed them inside. At the mezzanine level, the three left the elevator, Bardon leading the way to an office door upon which a brass plate proclaimed simply, DIRECTEUR.

In the hotel manager's outer office, Darnell and Penny listened as Bardon spoke in French to the pleasant, gray-haired receptionist. When he finished, she stood and offered Darnell and Penny a bright smile, saying in excellent, French-accented English, "Welcome, Professor Darnell. And Mrs. Darnell." She stepped over to the door to Bardon's private office and opened it.

Bardon bowed slightly, waved a hand of invitation, and Penny and John Darnell entered the office. The manager followed them and closed the door.

John Darnell, not unused to seeing luxurious fittings in his adventures aboard the *Titanic* and the Orient Express, raised his eyebrows nevertheless at the comforts of the manager's private office. The walls boasted original oil paintings, a plush white sofa sat against one wall facing a marble-topped table, and the room seemed nothing short of opulent, with an oversized mahogany desk and soft guest chairs facing it.

Bardon said, "I am very pleased you are here, Professor, and relieved. Holidays are here, and many celebrate now, after the war, but a hotel ghost dampens the spirits." He smiled. "My Chairman and I hope you can explain this quickly." He gestured toward the sofa. "Let us sit and talk. Would you like something to drink?"

Darnell glanced at Penny, who shook her head slightly, and he answered for them. "Nothing now. We'll have dinner soon."

"And I'll be your host. We have a special window table reserved, not too near the music, and yet not too far, overlooking the Champs-Elysees. Madame will enjoy it."

Penny smiled. "We'll enjoy all of Paris. It's so lovely."

A frown darkened Bardon's face. "It was lovelier before the war—but it will come back. Now, there are other matters . . ."

"Yes." Darnell's lips turned up. "The ghost."

Bardon's frown deepened. "I hope your smile is one of reassurance, Professor, because for six nights now guests have seen what they all swear is a ghost. Always on the ninth floor. Always near the Royal Suite 999. Always near midnight."

Darnell studied the manager, who seemed to become more overwrought with each word. "I'll need the facts of the murder of the American writer that Chairman Beauvais described to me."

Bardon nodded. "Yes. We're prepared to tell you everything. But as to the ghost—I am told it is the ghost of the murdered man, that it resembles him closely." He spread his hands wide. "But I have seen nothing myself." He paused. "It began this way. . . . The night of the great parades, Parisians carried their enthusiasm on well into the night with parties. Parties were held here in the hotel, especially in the large Royal Suites on each floor, such as Royal 999, where the death occurred."

"That room number—999?" Darnell mused. "So many rooms?"

"No, Professor. Le Grand has nine residence floors and a penthouse tenth, with a showroom and special rooms. Fourteen rooms and suites and a royal suite are on each of the nine floors. On nine, the numbers are 901 to 914, plus the Royal Suite, 999, kept for royalty when they are here, otherwise available upon reservation. And Tuesday last week, Eric Thorndyke was killed in that suite. Martin Prince's suite."

"He was strangled, your Chairman's telegram said."

Bardon shook his head. "Not strangled. Garroted, from all appearances. The thin, deep red marks on the throat . . ."

"The garrote. A strong, thin cord that with force embeds itself into the flesh." Darnell glanced at Penny, who frowned. He went on, "But that's a Spanish weapon—a murder or torture instrument invented and used in Spain, not France."

"Yes, exactly. Part of the mystery. But no weapon, no garrote, was found by the police. The case, of course, is under investigation by the *Sûreté*. They were called the first night."

"They interrogated everyone who attended the party?"

"*Oui*—oh, excuse me, I slip out of English."

"You speak it well."

"And German, and Spanish, and Italian. Paris is a cosmopolitan city. We have worldwide guests."

"And those at the party? Cosmopolitan also?"

He spread his hands. "French, English, American, Dutch. Even Spanish. A normal mixture for Paris, and Le Grand."

"Spanish . . . No doubt the police saw the connection there with the murder weapon—the garrote— and the Spanish guest?"

Bardon smiled. "The poor Spaniard. He was interrogated unmercifully. But as yet the *Sûreté* has no one person under suspicion. All are considered suspects and have been told not to leave Paris. In fact, Inspector Manot ordered those who had rooms here to stay in this hotel until the investigation is over."

"I'll need a list. I want to talk with them, one by one."

"I have a list, and repeat interviews have been scheduled for you by the Inspector, at the request of Chairman Beauvais. He is, as we say, close to those at the top of the *Sûreté*."

"The guests at that party—they were all in publishing? Writers, publishers, book dealers?"

Bardon turned up his nose and seemed to sniff. "Not exactly our type of clientele, you know. Not royalty or world leaders. But one is a noted young actress from America. Of course, their money is good."

"And you need to get new business, after the war."

"De rigueur. New business is essential, and they may stimulate it." He sighed. "I don't know how Le Grand survived the war. Half the Paris population was unemployed. Food and fuel were rationed. The main activity was troops marching off. There were no taxis. And we're only now getting clothes for fashion, instead of mourning clothes, in our shops." He handed Darnell a sheet of official-looking paper. "Here's the list."

Darnell glanced at the names. "And why were these people, these particular people, in Paris and here at this time?"

"There is a pent-up demand to see Paris and France. The war prevented it. The giant 'Big Bertha' cannon bombarded Paris, destroying buildings for months, from miles away. The shells could hit anywhere. Even as late as March, the war was just fifty miles from Paris. Some parts of the city were evacuated. And with the men gone, it has been a town for young widows."

Darnell nodded. "So, postwar enthusiasm starts already."

"The people at the party had come from Hollywood and New York, from London and Spain. Some of them are daring. Motion-picture producers. Publishers. Everyone seems to be looking for a new story, a new idea, a new market, now."

"M'sieur Bardon," Penny said, "tell me more about this apparition, what people call your 'ghost.'"

Bardon sighed. "It, or he, looks just like Eric Thorndyke from the descriptions given. Wearing exactly what he wore the night he died—a black tuxedo, red bow tie, patent-leather shoes, and a red cummerbund. Very bright look, very partylike. They were all dressed for the party that night, from what the waiters said. Men in their tuxedos or dinner jackets, women in their formal gowns. The champagne flowed freely, even by Paris standards." He smoothed back his shiny black hair. "A horrible murder in a party like that. No one could have expected it."

"Perhaps. But I find that murder seldom happens totally unexpectedly. Examine the people involved, their goals and motives and problems, and the killer will soon be revealed, as well as the reasons for the crime."

Bardon said, "Right now, it's the ghost that bothers me."

"And that's why I'm here, and where I'll start, tonight. Our room is on the ninth floor?"

"Room 914. Near suite 999."

"Excellent." Darnell rose. "Mr. Prince is in 999?"

"Yes, he's still there. Although no one uses the spare bedroom. The murdered man's son, Philip Thorndyke, is in room 913, next to you. He shared that smaller two-bedroom suite with his father, the victim, who had been living in London. Philip shipped the body back to America after the autopsy, but stays on, wanting the police to solve the crime. Thorndyke's wife died five years ago, and Philip was his only child."

Penny shook her head. "It must be hard on the young man. The last of his family."

"He hasn't left the suite since he sent off his father's body. We bring his meals up to him."

"Is he really waiting, or just following the *Sûreté*'s orders?" Darnell asked. "Waiting until they tell him he can leave?"

"No, he wants the crime solved. But he, especially, wants you to do whatever you can to clear up the mystery."

Darnell slipped the list into a pocket. "So we'll talk with all of them tomorrow. After dinner tonight, I'll prowl around the hotel, especially on the ninth floor. And, of course, you know where I'll be at midnight tonight."

Bardon nodded. "At room 999. *N'est-ce pas?*"

Chapter Two

Penny Darnell took in the surroundings of the restaurant, Armand's de Le Grand, as M'sieur Jacques Bardon led the way to the table he had reserved. As Bardon passed tables, several seated guests nodded at him, while others gazed at Penny with frank admiration and at Darnell with curiosity. Stories of the apparition at the hotel had spread by rumor, despite Bardon's efforts. And, of course, the murder of the writer rippled through conversations.

Bardon seated them, promising to return in a few moments. The window table indeed offered a panoramic view of the Champs-Elysees. As if on cue, dinner music resumed when the Darnells took their seats. Penny felt the eyes of guests at other tables resting upon her, inspecting her hair, her clothing, her subtle jewelry, the simple necklace and matching bracelet.

Penny looked about the ornate room at the other women, caught the gaze of one, nodded and smiled. She was glad she'd brought her violet evening dress, the one that matched her eyes, and at the moment she felt totally at ease. She turned her attention to her husband. If she felt it wouldn't distract him from his assignment, she would take this time before Bardon arrived to talk of some concerns she'd felt in London before they left for Paris, things that still worried her. And the talk about garrotes earlier had done nothing to ease her mind. But knowing her husband, she realized his thoughts were already focusing on his investigation, and he would soon become more distant as it proceeded.

She smiled. "You take me to the nicest places, John. I can't complain about that." She sighed. "But must there always be some sort of phantom, some murder, something deadly?"

"Deadly . . . yes, murders *are* rather deadly, my dear, by their nature," he said in an arch voice. She knew his moods, and could see he was determined not to be serious for a while. That would come, she knew. She'd enjoy him now, before events overtook them and thrust them into the middle of what no doubt would become chaos of a particularly dangerous nature.

Six years since she and John returned to England after surviving the tragedy of the *Titanic*'s sinking, and each of his cases seemed to take him deep into some maelstrom of deception. And this time, it all derived from an apparent apparition of the deceased. For a moment, she shivered, and pulled her black shawl closer about her shoulders. Had a cool breeze blown through the room?

"A penny for your thoughts, Penny."

Darnell's light tone refreshed her idea of enjoying the evening. What would come, would come. And the other things she wanted to talk about could wait. She smiled broadly at him. "I was just thinking, I'll get a chance to practice my French here."

"Good. Then you can order for us." Darnell turned his menu down with a flourish and beamed at her.

Bardon returned to the table and took a seat oppo-site Penny. "Now, we order champagne," he said.

A waiter arrived and showed the label of a cham-pagne bottle to Bardon. After Bardon nodded, the waiter filled his and Darnell's glasses. Penny took tea. Bardon said, "To cleanse the palate. We order wine later. I apologize for our limited carte—war shortages. We will have a better selection soon."

They sipped the champagne and glanced over the menus. Penny and Bardon talked about the room, the sparkling crystal in the chandelier overhead, the music of the small French band, the singer who mas-saged the senses of the audience with her dulcet voice. Darnell sat back, silent. Penny wondered if he'd slipped into his investigatory role, thinking about that list.

She turned to Bardon. "And Armand? Is he the chef?"

"No, he built Le Grand, twenty years ago, and owned it until the war closed it in 1916. A corpora-tion reopened it a year ago, after he died. We kept his name for the restaurant."

The waiter approached again, and Penny did as Darnell suggested. "*Nous voudrions—*" she began.

Darnell came back from his depths. "We'd like—"

Penny scowled at him. "Are you going to interpret everything I say?" She turned her attention to the menu and the waiter. "*Salade mêlée . . . bouillon de poule . . . saumon—poché . . . asperges.*"

The waiter said in English, "Very well, madame."

Darnell laughed lightly. "I'm glad he understood you. So we're having mixed salad, bouillon, poached salmon, and asparagus."

"Do you approve?"

"Most definitely."

Bardon ordered his dishes and a white wine for Darnell and himself with the food. As the courses came, they enjoyed the meal leisurely, commenting upon the music from time to time. Following coffee, Darnell made a show of looking at his watch. "After ten. We should be going. Things to do."

Bardon nodded and motioned to the waiter. "Come to my office in the morning at nine a.m. The Inspector will be there, and we can begin." He initialed the dinner check and rose.

"Leave the ninth floor to me tonight," Darnell said in a firm voice. "It's my job. I'll report to you on it tomorrow."

The young man, face unlined, not yet twenty by all appearances yet in the uniform of an American soldier, hobbled up to the front desk unselfconsciously on his hospital-issue crutches. Ernest Hemingway realized the stir he created as a wounded war hero. But he knew it was a choice of enduring the excess attention or, in fact, not being able to have this last holiday he had planned so carefully before his return to America.

His compatriots at the hospital in Italy thought he had taken the night train from Naples to visit Southern Italy, but he'd conspired to spend this last week in Paris. He smiled. What his buddies didn't know wouldn't hurt them, but what he missed at nineteen years of age could never be recaptured.

Hemingway greeted René Alain. "You have a room for me. I telegraphed last week. Hemingway, Ernest M."

Alain nodded, averting his eyes from the crutches.

He checked his records. "Yes, room 901. Do you have bags, sir?"

Hemingway jerked a thumb at a bellman standing next to a pillar with a suitcase in his case. "Just the one. He has it."

"Then sign here, and enjoy your stay. A week, I believe."

"Yes, until January second. After the New Year."

John Darnell stood in an alcove two dozen feet down from suite 999. This was the only place where he could be obscured and yet see the entire expanse of the corridor in either direction. He'd told Penny to keep the door locked to their room, 914, just next door to the suite, and that he'd let himself in with his key. Eleven forty-three, almost midnight, but for these last fifteen minutes, there had been no sign of life. Everyone on the floor seemed to be already in their rooms.

The elevator door opened with a light clang, and Darnell looked down at the other end of the hall. Only one man left the elevator, a young soldier on crutches. He stopped for a moment to get his bearings, then continued toward Darnell, looking at the numbers on the doors. Darnell's gaze was fixed on him as he wondered which room the man was heading toward. The man stopped again, a dozen or so feet away, staring past Darnell in the direction of Darnell's own room and suite 999.

"My God!" the soldier exclaimed. He balanced himself on one crutch and lifted the other, pointing down the hallway toward the suite. "Did you see that?" His question was aimed at Darnell.

Darnell whirled about and looked in the direction in which the soldier was pointing. Nothing there except a bit of odd haze, but the stairwell door swung gently back in place, and stopped.

The soldier hobbled over to Darnell. "It was a ghost, if you ask me," he said. "First it was there; then there was a little puff of smoke and it disappeared."

"Dammit! I missed him." Darnell ran down the corridor to the stairwell and burst through the doorway, looking down the stairs. Nothing there. He returned to the corridor.

The young soldier stood near the door, leaning forward on his crutches, his face showing his curiosity. "Did you see anything on the stairs?"

Darnell shook his head. "Your ghost is gone." He rubbed his forehead, thought for a moment, then asked, "What did he look like? Can you describe him?"

Ernest Hemingway nodded. "I'll try. It was some distance away, of course, and only for a few seconds. I wasn't expecting anything like that. Let me see . . . evening clothes, a tuxedo I think, a splash of red in his outfit, maybe his tie, and that thing they tie around their stomach—"

"Cummerbund."

"That's it."

"And the face?"

Hemingway grimaced. "I've seen the insides of more than a couple hospitals, and I've seen the faces of men there, walking ghosts of men, some not in their own minds anymore. But this face—his face—" He shuddered. "Like a ghost, as I said. Pasty white, that's all I can tell you. A very white ghostly face."

Chapter Three

Darnell smiled at his wife. "Three cups of coffee helped. I'm awake now." He set the room-service tray aside.

Penny Darnell sat at the dressing table putting finishing touches on her wardrobe and appearance. She brushed her long hair with rhythmic strokes. "Should I go with you to meet with the manager this morning?"

"Yes, but I know you want to see more of Paris this trip than we did the last time. Let's see how deep the meeting goes." He paused. "And today, while I talk with those who were in the party last week when the man was killed—"

She put in, "I'll be at the Louvre or the Tuileries."

He told her about the "ghost" sighting and the soldier as he finished his shaving and dressing routine. Thirty minutes later he and Penny entered the outer office of Jacques Bardon.

When the receptionist looked up at them, Darnell saw a subtle difference in her expression. A new element?

"The *Directeur* is waiting for you. Inspector Manot is with him and is anxious to meet you."

Darnell and Penny exchanged glances. She spoke first. "I'll excuse myself after we meet him. I just remembered some shopping I should do." Her eyes twinkled.

He smiled, and they stepped into Bardon's office. Bardon rose from the sofa where he and Inspector Manot sat and walked toward them, shaking Darnell's hand, greeting Penny with a smile, and saying, "Professor, Mrs. Darnell—Inspector Louis Manot."

Darnell sized up Manot as much as possible in a glance—a trim, modestly dressed man somewhat older than his own thirty-seven years, perhaps in his early fifties, with gray around the temples taking over the black, but the hair still thick and unruly. A pipe stuck out of the breast pocket of his coat. "Inspector Manot, very pleased indeed. This is my wife, Penny."

Manot smiled in return. "*Bonjour*. And welcome to Paris." His accent was Parisian but understandable. "I speak your language, Professor, but not always *a coup sur*. Do not hesitate to correct me, or ask twice for the right answer."

"You studied in England?"

"Yes. Your Cambridge. Basics. English for the foreigner."

"And I've spent time at your Sorbonne, teaching psychology and philosophy."

Manot smiled. "The English think deep thoughts."

"As do the French."

Penny coughed lightly. "Gentlemen—if you will excuse me, I have some shopping to do this morning." She touched Darnell's arm lightly. "Then I'll see you in our room, say, about one?"

He nodded. "Good. Then lunch."

As she left the office, Bardon gestured toward the

sofa and nearby chairs. "Inspector Manot will bring you up to date, Professor, and tell you what we've planned for the morning."

Manot's expression changed as they seated themselves. Gone was the casual tone he used in Penny's presence. "*Mon Dieu!* I understand why the hotel employed you to investigate. Criminals I can deal with; ghosts, no. But you need to understand the division between what you will do and our police procedures."

Darnell sensed a bit of territorial jealousy on Manot's part, although the man seemed pleasant enough. Probably resented this secondary investigation after having done his own a week earlier. "You, ah, have no clues, as I understand it, as to Mr. Thorndyke's killer—except the garrote. Perhaps a fresh round of interrogations with your second look at things may flush him out."

Manot's voice did not soften. "I will lead any talks whenever our jurisdiction is involved. And I need to know anything you learn in any way."

Darnell met the other's eyes. "Of course, I understand perfectly." He paused. "The garrote is a particularly vicious way of performing a killing. The victim struggles within the killer's own hands, twisting, trying to breathe, perhaps striking out, but always with one end in mind—to get that tight, strangling cord from around his neck."

Manot nodded. "You describe it with perfection. To use a garrote, one must kill '*a froid*'—in cold blood, as the English and Americans say. No feelings must be allowed to interfere during that minute of violent death."

Darnell pulled out the list of the party guests Bardon had given him the night before. "Your office prepared this list, Inspector. I see there was one guest at the party who seems to be from Spain." He read the name. "Ricardo Camilo."

"A writer from Spain, meeting with Martin Prince, who called the conference."

Darnell scanned down the list. "Martin Prince— Editorial Director of an American publisher, as it says here."

"We determined that almost everyone at the party had come here from other places to see *M'sieur*—that is, Mr. Prince," Manot said. "It was like a command performance. And, yes, we spoke with the Spaniard first. That would be most obvious, *n'est-ce pas*? A Spanish garrote as the weapon? We could prove nothing on Camilo. We also interrogated the other guests. As M'sieur Bardon tells, they all had the connection with Mr. Prince." He sighed. "We've done everything—but we'll do it again—for your Chairman Beauvais."

Darnell nodded. "He wants the hotel rid of the ghost." He turned to Bardon. "Are all those at the party still registered in the hotel?"

"All except one woman, a Sylvia Beach, who has her own apartment in Paris not far from here."

Manot said, "My specific orders to them are to stay in Paris. My rule is *de rigueur*. Until they are completely cleared, they are still suspect."

"Mr. Bardon said you had laid out a schedule for our talks today, Inspector?"

"We go to the rooms of as many of the suspects— the guests—as we can." He handed Darnell another sheet.

"A dozen on your list."

"The murdered man would have made it thirteen. An unlucky number, it would seem."

Darnell frowned. "Only because a murderer made it such."

Bardon rose. "Shall we start, then? I'll go along as the hotel representative. My Chairman would want nothing less. After all, we are paying for this round." He smiled at Darnell. "And the ghost? Did you see any trace of it last night?"

As the three men walked from the office and down the corridor to the elevators, Darnell told Bardon and Manot of the experience he and the young soldier shared just before midnight. "I took the soldier's name and room number. He's on the ninth floor also. He may be of some use later for identification, if it comes to that. Seemed to be very alert, although somewhat disabled from his war wounds."

"Identification is what we need, as you say," Manot groaned, "and very soon. Or my Chief Inspector will do more than blow pipe smoke at me and give me the reprimand in his office." He passed a stern look at Darnell and added, "So let us see what the world's only paranormal detective can do."

The three entered the elevator and Bardon told the operator, "Nine, Josef, si'l vous plaît."

Ernest Hemingway considered the idea of traversing the corridor to the elevators with his cane, leaving the crutches in his room. "I can do this," he said aloud in the otherwise vacant corridor. "I *have* to do it. Can't be a damned cripple all my life."

A classically handsome and well-dressed woman stepping out of her room just at that moment heard the last bit of his words, but pretended not to hear. She walked with her head down, fussing with her purse, also heading toward the elevator. Inevitably,

they both took the same elevator down to the main
floor.

As the elevator descended she spoke to Hemingway. "You ver in ze var?"

To his ears, her accent sounded German—he'd heard
prisoners speak—but thought she must be Dutch. No
Germans could be in Paris this soon after the war.

He laughed sardonically. "Yes, I was. As a writer,
I'd call it a passive verb, but the war wasn't passive."
He relented his cynical tone. After all, this was his
vacation. He must learn to lighten his attitude, stop
suspecting people, try to get back to a normal view
before returning to the states. "I, ah, was struck by
shrapnel in the legs. Drove ambulances in Italy."

She looked down. "I am sorry. I hope you recover soon."

"I'm working on it." He forced a laugh. "Putting
my best foot forward." He smiled at his own joke.

"I am Edda Van Eych, from Holland," she said.
"Not German."

"I see." He looked at her more closely—a youngish
forty, he speculated. Hair very dark, eyes of green,
with the look of a professional about her, or an ac-
complished secretary. And yet, she had a hard edge
to her, perhaps from her war experiences.

"I am a writer," she went on. "I write ze book
about ze war, try to have it published in America."
She paused. "You—you are American, is it not so?"

"Yes. The vanishing American." He smiled. "Vanishing into Paris for a last gasp of Europe before
going home."

The elevator reached the ground floor, and the two
exited as the operator pulled the door back for them.

"I vill see you, perhaps, later? I hope you—"

"Recover. Yes, thank you. I plan to do just that."

Hemingway stared at the woman as she strode away toward the front entrance. A determined type, a strong-willed Dutch woman. He frowned. If she *was* really Dutch . . . Could he use her in a story? *I should take notes*, he thought. *I could meet some intriguing characters in Paris—even in this hotel.*

As the young man slowly moved with the aid of his cane across the lobby toward a chair by the window, a girl seated on a sofa followed him with her blue-eyed gaze. Mary Miles Minter shook her mop of wavy, brilliant golden hair to emphasize her words to her mother, and frowned petulantly. "War is real over here. Not like in my movies."

Charlotte Shelby gave something close to a snort and responded, "Nothing is like it is in the movies, dear. You have to learn that."

The blond girl shook her curls again. "I've seen some men who lost a leg or an arm. And him—I saw him come in on crutches last night. He was really wounded, too. Poor soldier. And so young."

Her mother gazed at her daughter. "At sixteen, you don't know much of life. He could be eighteen or twenty-two. How could you tell?"

"He's nice looking . . . and I'll be seventeen real soon. And then eighteen, and pretty soon, twenty-one. An *adult*."

Charlotte Shelby scowled at her. "Don't yearn to be an adult that soon, and don't worry about your money, if that's what you're driving at, young lady. You know I'm managing that very well. Who else could get you a contract for twenty pictures and over a million dollars?" Charlotte Shelby took a deep breath and went on. "I'll tell you who—your own mother." As she reigned in her emotions, her voice softened. "Enjoy being sixteen, dear. You only get that chance one time." She took out a compact and inspected her face in the small mirror, frowned, and snapped it shut again.

"I wonder what William's doing," Mary Miles Minter said. She stared into space with a dreamy quality in her expression; then her eyes widened. "Probably with that Mabel Normand woman. I hate her!" She shook her head in anger, curls bobbing.

"You're better off without him. He's forty if he's a day."

"I think—I mean I *thought*—I loved him."

"You mean until Mabel came along."

"Yes. Then I hated him! I still hate him." Tears came into her eyes and she brushed them away.

"We came over here to get away from Hollywood, Mary—from him, and from all that for a while, to get things straight in our minds. You have to go back and do twenty pictures in five years. And you'll still be only twenty-one when they're finished."

"You think I can't do it? I just finished twenty-six pictures."

Charlotte Shelby clucked her tongue at her daughter, as she often did. "But these are *real* pictures. At Paramount Studios."

Mary Minter stared into space. "William will direct me."

Her mother nodded, unsmiling. "Some of them, yes. He's under contract there. But he'd better keep his hands off you. No one is going to bother my baby girl again. When we go back, we go strong, Mary. No one stops us. We get our million dollars plus, and you'll never have to worry about money again."

Mary Miles Minter smiled sweetly at her mother.

"And neither will you—right, Mother? Isn't that really it?"

Her mother did not respond, but instead stood. "I'm going to talk with that clerk at the front desk again. Stay here."

Mary knew what that was all about—wanting permission to leave Paris, throwing around her influence, the influence that being the mother of a famous actress gave her. Her mother wanted to get away from the cloud of suspicion the murder had created. She shivered, remembering that night, the questioning by the Inspector, and his orders not to leave Paris. Well, for her part, she had no urge to return to America until after the New Year began. She wanted to be on the Champs-Elysees on New Year's Eve, welcoming in the year 1919—a year she considered the most important in her young life—and then return to Hollywood.

Mary's thoughts moved on. She gazed about the room. That young man, that American soldier, she wondered about him. Her sixteen-year-old heart beat a little more rapidly as she studied him and observed the expression on his face. There was something about him.

She watched as the young soldier rose from his seat by the window and headed back through the lobby again. He was walking, it seemed, directly toward her, although she suspected he was headed toward the brasserie. She took special notice of his face, which, she felt, had a sweet although pained look about it. Pain from his legs, of course.

A mischievous thought, not uncommon for Mary, flashed in her mind. She would test him, and test his legs and determination. She rose and walked toward him with her purse open, rummaging in it, allowing a delicate handkerchief to float down to the floor as if unaware of it falling, and then continuing on slowly for a few steps, stopping, looking in her purse, giving him the bait. He took it.

"Oh, miss," the soldier called to her, "your handkerchief."

Mary Miles Minter turned back toward him, looked demurely at her open purse, then returned the few steps toward him. Somehow he had managed, as she had seen in her side vision, to stoop down and retrieve the bit of silk cloth from the marble floor. He had passed her test. She stepped close to him and looked up at his height of six feet or more from her own vantage point of an inch more than five feet. Her crystal blue eyes met his, and she gave him her best smile, one that millions of people had seen on the screen in dark theaters.

"Thank you, sir," she said. "You have very sharp eyes."

Something brought a bright smile to his face, and Mary knew what would come next—an invitation of some kind, a question, an effort to get to know her. And that was precisely what she now wanted. Him to know her, she to know him. She glanced at her mother again, still talking, and waited for the soldier to speak.

Penny Darnell stopped as she left the elevator and glanced about the wide expanse of Le Grand's lobby. She knew shops offering ladies' garments, coiffures, and facials were in prominent, convenient spots on the mezzanine, but just now she wanted to get outdoors, into Paris.

A book and curio shop to her left caught her attention, and she decided to get a tourist map there. She walked purposefully to the shop, stepped inside, and glanced about at the souvenirs, books, and newspapers. A rack of maps sat against the far wall, and she moved toward it. Coming from the other direction in the narrow aisle, a woman brushed against her arm awkwardly and dropped the selection of magazines and books she was carrying.

"Oh, I'm so sorry," Penny said, and stooped to help the woman retrieve her selections.

"No, no, it was my fault—looking one way, walking another. My mind was far away." She bent down and picked up the remaining books and took the magazines Penny returned to her. She looked at Penny and smiled. "American, aren't you?"

Penny nodded. "Yes, originally. I live in London now, with my husband. We're here on his business."

"I'm Sylvia Beach. Yankee, too. Princeton."

"Penny Darnell. Texas. At least, I was born there. I lived in New York up until six years ago."

The two stood looking at each other. Penny, taller than the slight framed woman with bobbed hair, felt the other was a few years older than herself. But she was an American, and a friendly one.

Penny ventured a thought about her mission. "I was looking for a good tourist map. Do you know Paris?"

Sylvia Beach nodded. "I've lived here more or less on my own quite a lot. I have an apartment not too far from here, in fact. I find my way around." She stepped over to the rack and took a colorful map from its holder. "You might try this one." She eyed Penny. "You're going out today?"

"Yes. John—my husband—has business all morning."

The other woman's voice was eager. "Then let me introduce you to my Paris. I'm always proud to show her off."

"But your books?"

"I'll leave them at the counter and pick them up later."

Penny felt charmed by the other's openness. "You're staying here, at Le Grand?"

"Not really. I have my own place, as I said. I did stay in a room last Tuesday—police were questioning people all night. I'll tell you more about it if we . . ." She looked at Penny.

"Sounds mysterious. Well, we're staying in 914." Penny decided. "Yes, let's see Paris. I've got until one o'clock."

Penny bought her map and stood back while Sylvia Beach explained to the clerk that she'd return later to purchase the books and magazines she handed her. The two walked to the front exit, out into the stark sunshine and cool, crisp air, and onto the busy sidewalks of the wide and beautiful boulevard Champs-Elysees.

Chapter Four

John Darnell stood aside with Inspector Manot as *Directeur* Bardon rapped on the door of room 912 for their appointment with Martin Prince's close associate, Patricia August—the first of the guests at the party at which Thorndyke was murdered. Darnell hoped to soon find out what each knew or suspected about the ghost sighting, and how it might be related to the death of the writer.

A woman in her mid-thirties with a single streak of white in her long black hair, opened the door partway and, upon seeing Bardon, swung it fully open. "Come in. I was expecting you. I ordered up coffee."

She gestured toward the seating, sofas and chairs opposite a table on which rested a silver coffeepot and several cups, sugars, and creams. She bent over the table and coffeepot.

The men seated themselves. Darnell looked about, noticing a Remington typewriter and a stack of paper. An editor's room. He watched her as she filled their cups. She finished, looked expectantly at first Bardon, then Manot, and finally, with obvious curiosity, at the man she knew only as Professor Darnell.

Manot spoke first. "It is not our intention to burden you, Miss August, with repetition. Professor Darnell is here as, ah, a specialist dealing with the unusual phenomenon seen here."

Patricia August favored them with a sardonic smile. "The ghost. Yes, I've heard." She took a cigarette from the gold-filigreed box on the table and held the box out to the others. Bardon produced a lighter and held it to the tip of her cigarette. She puffed quickly and blew smoke toward the ceiling, then drew in smoke again deeply. "Terrible habit," she said. "One of many."

Darnell was unsurprised at her nervousness. No doubt everyone they interviewed would be on edge. "Did you see the ghost yourself?"

"No, not I. But several others did."

"Looking like Eric Thorndyke?"

"Looking as he might look if dead. That's how Edda Van Eych put it. She said she saw the—thing—Christmas Eve." Then after another puff, "But she is, I'd say, an imaginative writer. I frankly don't know what to make of this, nor does Mr. Prince."

"I wonder, Miss August, as a close associate editor for Mr. Prince, if you could give me some background on these meetings. Why he wanted to initiate them, why here in Paris, why now, and why these particular guests? Anything you can offer."

She looked at Manot, who scowled, but nodded, then returned her gaze to Darnell. "You'll be talking with Mr. Prince soon, I'm sure, and he'll speak for himself. But, if it will save him some time . . ." She ground her cigarette out in an ashtray. "The meeting was planned to be an annual affair, the first of many. Paris seemed to be an inspiring place for the first one, Mr. Prince felt. Some authors were here on the Continent, and people he wanted to see were in England. The war just over, rebirth of Europe, renewal, all of that." She gestured toward the windows through which the Eiffel Tower could be seen in the distance. "No place more inspirational for a writer."

"Mr. Thorndyke, the victim? Tell me what you know of him."

She nodded. "He was from America, but had lived in London since his wife died. He'd written books, but turned to motion-picture production in Hollywood. He still traveled there, and to New York to meet with Mr. Prince, while the shipping lanes were open. He had grand ideas, thinking ahead. And his son—well, he had stayed in Hollywood. He came over on the ship we all took."

"Who would want to kill Eric Thorndyke?"

"The inevitable question. The Inspector knows every answer each of us has given." She sighed. "But I'll repeat mine. No one. He was rather aggressive with his ideas. He drank too much. Basically harmless, not a threat. Not like his son."

Darnell met her gaze steadily. "His son—you opened that door. Please continue with that."

"Philip Thorndyke. Not dry behind his ears, but full of himself. An egoist, with a dangerous combination of major ambitions and minor talents."

"Is he a writer?"

"He tries to match his father's writing skill and reputation. Of course, he's in his mid-twenties, and has a lot ahead of him. I'll give him this much. . . . Like all sons of famous fathers, he has a great hurdle to get over in trying to achieve his own success, because people expect more of him. He's probably trying too hard."

"He's always been overshadowed by his father?"

"Yes. And he didn't like that much."

"And now his father is dead."

She looked at him and Manot. "I'm sure you can find many motives here, if you turn over all the rocks."

Darnell was anxious to talk with Martin Prince now, the next on the list. His associate was open, but not expansive. Prince might have more to say. The three men stepped next door to room 999. As Manot rapped on the door, Darnell spoke in a low voice to Bardon. "Perhaps we should have used the connecting door between the two rooms. Very convenient for them."

Bardon smiled. "We try to accommodate."

A booming voice called out, "Come in." Darnell opened the door, and as they stepped in he saw that the room was truly royal, much larger than his own, with living room, kitchen, and dining room, a spacious bedroom whose door stood open revealing a four-poster bed with a canopy, and a second closed door—the bedroom in which the murder took place. An ebony grand piano centered in the living room dominated, despite the competing attractions of original oil paintings on the walls, the thick shag carpet, and the fringed Tiffany floor lamps.

Darnell thought, wryly, despite whatever deficiencies the hotel had—such as the occasional murder—the suite's fittings and furnishings were magnificent. *Yes, a lovely place in which to die!*

He glanced at Bardon. "This is where the party took place?"

"Yes. Prince had commandeered the largest royal suite. I think he wanted it because he had planned ahead to have the party here. All our suites, such as yours, are comfortable and almost as large. The Thorndyke suite has two equal bedrooms, needed for father and son, more appropriate for them."

A man several inches shorter than Darnell's six feet and slender, almost to the point of looking underfed, entered the living room from the open bedroom door. He wore a burgundy dressing gown with a white scarf at the neck, appearing as if he had just arisen. His unruly brown hair showed tinges of gray, and Darnell felt it looked as if he combed it only on rare occasions, this not one of them. The striped gray trousers below the robe were sharply creased, and his black boots were highly polished.

Martin Prince's deep voice, the one that had called to them to enter, coming from such a slight frame surprised Darnell. "Gentlemen. Take seats. Please." Prince flopped in a soft chair opposite their seats. "Damned nasty thing, this. I haven't decided yet whether it's good for business or not. Might sell more of Thorndyke's other books in a spurt, now. But what a horrible way to die." He ran a finger around the edge of the scarf. "The Spaniard, I'd say, probably did it. A garrote—a Spanish thing, isn't it? And a hothead, too. But naturally we defer to the authorities to investigate." He looked at Darnell pointedly. "And now we have another authority here."

Manot did the formal introduction. "Professor Darnell, M'sieur Martin Prince." Darnell took Prince's outstretched hand. Thin and bony, the hand was moist from perspiration. Inspector Manot made opening remarks to Prince about Darnell's purposes.

"Yes, yes, I know all that," Prince said. "*Directeur* Bardon told me he was coming." He studied Darnell. "Ever thought of writing a book about your experiences, Professor? The supernatural? Séances? Your experiences with that sort of thing? I'd be happy to handle it for you. Might go over big in America, and we have London outlets. Much interest in that."

John Darnell did not smile in return. Wasn't it just last week Penny had asked him the same question? "Thank you, but I'm not ready to do my memoirs yet. Now, Mr. Prince, I'd appreciate your commenting about the meetings you called and your invited guests. Can you give me a quick sketch of them?"

"A thumbnail sketch. All right." He spoke of Eric Thorndyke and his son, Philip, echoing the remarks of Patricia August. "The Spaniard, I might as well tell you, is not my favorite of the group. Ricardo Camilo's first book did not sell well. I told him last week the chances of a new contract, unless he had something terrific this time, were slim. So, he's been bad-mouthing my firm and me."

Darnell glanced at the list Bardon had given him. "Brandon Tyler? Is he another publisher? A competitor?"

"No, no. He's our London contact. Publishes for us in England." He paused. "Hasn't done much lately with the war, of course, but now that it's over—well, I'm looking for a rejuvenation of publishing, not only in America but here on the Continent and in England. I hope old Tyler is up to it. We may have to look about a bit."

"Who else is here, at your invitation, and was at the party the night Eric Thorndyke was killed?" Darnell kept an eye on his list, preparing for Prince's remarks.

"There's Sylvia Beach, nice young woman. She's spent some time on the Continent, mostly here in Paris, and wants to open a bookstore. Intelligent. Lots of drive. She was at the party at my invitation. Then there's David L. Fitch and his gorgeous wife, Cynthia—'Filthy-Rich Fitch' I call him. Made his money on munitions. He's here mainly, I think, to buy properties."

"Real estate? Then why see you?"

"I say mainly. He has so much money he wants to put some of it in motion pictures in Hollywood. Producing, I suppose. Maybe buying a studio. He and Thorndyke had several private meetings. And he likes the idea of publishing, becoming a kingmaker for authors. I humor him. With his millions, I have to. Who knows, he might even buy my firm someday."

"The party was held Tuesday night, December seventeenth. When did you and the other guests arrive?"

"Over the three or four days before that, drifting in. Some on the oceanliner we took from America. The rest by train from various points over here or a boat across the channel. I met with each of them, and some met with one another for mutual interests, but it was my party last Tuesday that brought them all together for the first time in the same room."

"Who else is in your group?"

"There's Bert Ward, works for Fitch and his wife. A general flunky, with maybe a bit of bodyguard thrown in. And Edda Van Eych. I'm looking over her book, but frankly . . ."

Manot suggested, "And, of course, the young actress . . ."

"Oh yes, Mary Miles Minter, not over seventeen, and her doting if not dotty mother, Charlotte Shelby. The Shelby woman heard Fitch was going to be here and got herself invited. She smells money, just like how she wangled that million-dollar motion-picture contract for her daughter. Of course, the daughter's pretty as a picture herself, a sweet young thing. She'd look as great on a book jacket as she does on the screen. I'm looking into that. The mother? Butter wouldn't melt in her mouth. But we'll still talk about a book."

"What do you know about this ghost?"

Prince shook his head. "Some claim to have seen it, even some of the authors here, other guests. I've seen nothing."

Darnell and Manot exchanged glances. Darnell felt he had enough to begin. He tucked his list back in his pocket.

They thanked Martin Prince for his help. Manot said to Prince, "We hope to have this all settled in a few days." He glanced at Darnell, then turned back to Prince with an explanation, anticipating the question he had been asked by others, why no one in the group could leave Paris.

Prince shook his head. "No rush. I wouldn't leave now, if I could. I'll celebrate New Year's Eve atop the Eiffel Tower."

Evidently, Darnell thought wryly, a strangulation murder had done little to dampen Martin Prince's spirits. An aggressive editor, the man was probably studying possibilities of a mystery story about Thorndyke's murder. Maybe *Death by Garrote*.

"The actress next?" Darnell looked at Manot and Bardon as they walked down the hall.

Manot answered with some pique. "It's my schedule, and we'll stay with it. The young man, Philip Thorndyke, is number three on the list. I've put them in the order I thought best, knowing what I know after our first interview. And I've had each of them advised to be ready at a specific time."

"Thank you. I'll follow your list, Inspector. How is the young man managing to deal with the murder of his father and the aftermath?"

Bardon answered, "It has been ten days. The body has been shipped off. He seems to want only two things—to be left alone in his suite, and to see the murderer caught. That's all he talks about. And, of course, his father's ghost."

The young Thorndyke opened the door of the suite, and at his invitation, they took seats on a sofa, he sitting opposite them, so he could speak to all three of them at once. But his eyes fixed on Darnell.

"I hope you can add to this investigation, Professor Darnell," Philip Thorndyke said. "I know you've been brought here because of the ghost thing, but I want the murderer of my father brought to justice." He looked down, seeming to study the laces on his shoes for a moment, then raised his narrowed eyes to Darnell's. "I don't want to interfere with police procedures—although I must say they've found nothing yet. I'll pay whatever it takes for you to find the killer. Over and above whatever arrangement you have with the hotel, you understand. I want you to know that." His forehead remained furrowed in a deep frown.

Darnell felt the man's emotion was genuine, but with everyone in the Prince group either producing fiction or acting, he sensed that all of them were putting on an act, that things were left unsaid, and information couldn't be taken at face value. He'd have to find a way to cut through all that. The son offered the most likely prospect to reveal motives. And he could describe, if he would, the discovery of his father's body and its condition.

Darnell said, "Thank you for that offer. We all want the same things here. What would help me the most now, would be to get a complete description of what happened that night, the night your father died. The party, how your father acted, and even the description of what you found, although that might be painful."

Philip Thorndyke sat back in his chair, closed his eyes, and frowned. When he opened them, Darnell saw in them a determination to do what he must, however painful it might be.

"The night of the party was not all sweetness and light, although some might like you to believe that." The young man stared at the wall beyond Darnell's head as if focusing his mind on the scene a week earlier. "Champagne, caviar, yes. The usual trappings. A pianist to play in Prince's suite, of course."

"But not all pleasant?"

"An undercurrent, I'd say. It seems everyone there wanted something, but no one was at all sure he would get it. The whole thing was Martin Prince's idea. Shake the tree, and see what falls out."

"And what did?"

Thorndyke took a deep breath. "My father. He had another of his great ideas going. Wouldn't tell me much about it, but I'm sure a few others had heard— Prince at least. Then the Dutch lady. She'd been told her new book wasn't up to Prince's standards. I overheard her talking to someone about that."

"Who?"

"The Spaniard, Camilo. He had the same problem. They were commiserating with each other. Maybe doing more than that."

"Go on."

"Trisha—Patricia August—was happy enough. Hanging on Prince's arm most of the time, although I don't see the attraction there. Fitch, the millionaire, was everywhere, rubbing up against the young actress, touching her, you know. Even caressing her mother's arm. Checking the merchandise. His wife was fuming underneath; I could see that. Tyler, the Englishman, seemed worried about renewing his contract to publish books from Prince's firm, in London."

Darnell's eyes glistened. "You, ah, didn't miss much."

"I'm a writer. A writer observes. You wanted them all? Well, Sylvia Beach, the American woman who lives in Paris, talked with Prince about a bookshop. And Ward, Fitch's man of some sort, slunk around, keeping to himself—not drinking much, and quiet. Observing, like I was doing."

"Let's talk about your father, if you can. I understand he excused himself with a headache."

Philip Thorndyke nodded. "He'd been drinking too much. It was noisy, with the piano tempo picking up as the party wore on, people talking louder. My father went into Prince's spare bedroom." He stopped for a moment, seeming to seek more strength.

"Are you comfortable with this?" Darnell asked gently.

The young man waved a hand in the air. "The party went on. Some singing. Prince was holding forth on the future of publishing after the war. Pie in the sky, I thought. After maybe an hour I went in to see if my father needed anything and found him sprawled at all angles in the chair, head to one side, that deep, bloody cut in his neck, his eyes bulging—God!" He shuddered. "I checked for a pulse, but he was gone."

"Others came into the room then?"

"I came out, cried out—they started streaming around. I said something like, 'Get away—call the police'—words like that. And I stayed there with my father's body until the hotel physician, Dr. Pascal, came up with Mr. Bardon. Then we waited together until the Inspector, here, arrived an hour later."

"Do you have any idea at all who might have killed him?"

"None. He was no saint, my father, but . . ."

"The bedroom he was in has a door that leads out to the hotel corridor. Was that the probable access for the killer?"

"I'd have seen anyone enter from the living room."

"Who left the suite after your father initially retired to that room?"

"Anyone and everyone. The main door to the suite was being opened and closed all the time. People were going back to their own rooms, then returning, sometimes two leaving for a private discussion—or whatever. I left myself, actually, to go down to the lobby to get some cigarettes. And Mr. Bardon, here, came up to wish us well once, during the party."

"Now, they say the ghost looks exactly like your father."

Thorndyke seemed to study the carpet at his feet. "It's too gruesome. I've seen nothing, but I don't doubt the word of the others. I hope you can clear that up—that would be part of my offer."

"All right," Darnell said. "Well, I have enough for now. But I'd like to see your father's bedroom. It looks like it's situated similar to that spare room in Prince's suite."

The son stood, crossed the room, opened a bedroom door, and was followed in by Darnell and the others. "His room."

Darnell stepped over to the outer door, opened it, and peered out into the corridor. He examined the handle on the door and the locking device, which twisted in one direction to lock it and another to unlock it. "I assume the room in Prince's suite is similar," he said to Manot. "I'd like to examine it sometime. That bedroom outer door could have been unlocked, or Thorndyke could have opened it to someone who might have knocked on it, and allowed that person to enter," he mused. "Someone he knew."

The three thanked Philip Thorndyke, left him in his suite, and stood for a moment outside in the corridor. Bardon excused himself, saying he must return to the office, and that Darnell and Manot should carry on.

Manot said, "We haven't found out much yet."

"I was surprised he didn't show much concern about the ghost sightings, more of an afterthought." Darnell glanced at his watch. He thought of Penny and wondered where she was. Suddenly he felt a flicker of concern for her, although he knew it was irrational. He knew she could take care of herself, but in a strange city . . . ? A vision of someone tightening a garrote around the neck of Eric Thorndyke flashed in his mind. He shook his head and took a deep breath.

"Not yet noon," he said. "We've got time for one more before lunch. Who's next on your list?"

Chapter Five

Friday, late morning, December 27

"She seems to be looking right into my eyes," Penny said. "You wonder what she's thinking, and why that enigmatic smile is on her lips."

"The Mona Lisa . . . _La Gioconda_ in Italian, _La Joconde_ in French. It means 'lighthearted woman.' " Sylvia Beach spoke with pride to her newfound friend. She wondered at times like this what it was about Paris that captivated her, an American, and made her feel part of it. "Yes, _La Joconde_ looks at you, Penny, and maybe into your heart or soul, depending on how profound you feel it."

"The painting is smaller than I thought it would be."

"The size surprises everyone. Less than two feet wide by three feet tall. But inch for inch, it's the most famous painting in the world."

"I can see why. I love it. Her smile's so mysterious." Penny glanced at her watch. "Thanks for the guided tour. I can tell John I've seen the Champs-Elysees Boulevard and Palais du Louvre already. So—would you like to have tea? I'll buy."

"I'd love to. Come with me." Sylvia took Penny to

a corner of the main-floor lobby where they bought tea and took their cups to one of the small round tables.

As they settled in, Penny said, "Maybe you can tell me now why you come to Le Grand when you have your own apartment in Paris. Your little mystery."

Sylvia nodded. She had no reservations about talking with Penny, and in fact wanted to tell someone. What was it her mother always said? *It takes two people to keep one secret.*

Penny poured milk into her tea, British style. "I'm listening."

Sylvia began, feeling relieved hearing her own words tumble out. "A man was murdered at a party I attended at Le Grand last Tuesday. And the *Sûreté* told everyone at the party he wanted to question us all that night, so I had to stay on. They seemed to consider us all suspects. Of course, the others were all registered there. The questioning wasn't over until after three a.m., so they gave me a room to stay in that night."

"That was Eric Thorndyke's murder, wasn't it?"

"What? How did you know?"

"That's why my husband is here. Professor John Darnell. He's looking into some aspects of it."

Sylvia Beach stared at her companion. "My God! I didn't know his name. Doesn't he investigate the sightings of ghosts? I heard he was called a 'psychichologist,' or something like that."

Penny laughed. "That's a name he created for his work. Yes, what he does is show that ghosts and supernatural events that seem to be real aren't real at all."

Sylvia nodded. "Thorndyke's ghost. A number of people have seen it." She shuddered. "He seems to be at large at midnight."

"And the dead man, his body—you saw it?"

"I'll never forget it. I took one look and turned away. The hotel manager and the doctor came up and took over. Then the Inspector. Then the questioning."

"Maybe I shouldn't ask this, but do you have any ideas about who did it or why?"

"I'll leave that to the police. But I can tell you this much." She looked at an older couple at the next table, leaned forward, and lowered her voice. "There was no love lost in that room that night, and after the champagne started flowing, the talk was quite loose. It was like everyone had something against at least one other person there."

"Enough for murder?"

"That's something your husband may be able to answer. What I felt before the murder, I'm not sure anymore. But afterward, I couldn't sleep that night, lying there in that hotel room on the same floor, thinking about the vibrations I felt in that room. It was like a *danse macabre*—a dance of death."

Mary Miles Minter flashed her smile, worth over a million dollars in Hollywood, across the table at the soldier, who was now, to her, simply Ernest. And she spoke his name, merely because she wanted to hear the word come from her own lips. "Ernest . . . that's a nice name."

He drank from his mug of beer and glanced around the room at the other customers. "Thanks. I like your name, Mary Miles Minter. Three M's. Easy to remember." He paused, looking at her. "We were born in different centuries," he said, "weren't we? Me in the nineteenth, you in the twentieth."

"Please, Ernest, if you're trying to find out my age, don't bother. No one can know. Hollywood stuff. If no one knows my age, I can play a woman from eighteen to twenty-five."

"Closer to the former than the latter, I'm sure."

"How would you know about age? You must be the youngest American soldier in Paris today."

"I don't know. I was the youngest in my Italian hospital. Really, just a Red Cross driver."

"You're out of the army now. Why don't you come to California, to Hollywood? There are good jobs there for writers. You said you wanted to write."

He stiffened. "I do write, already. I worked for a newspaper for six months. I have lots of ideas."

"I'm sure." As she sipped her sarsaparilla, she studied his face and saw the pride there. "Tell me some of them."

"A movie star wouldn't be interested."

"I am. Please."

He rubbed his chin. "Well, I want to come back to Paris someday, after I get my bearings and get my legs back. I'd like to live over here somewhere and scout around Europe. Spain. See the bullfights, you know. Things like that. And then write about them. And, of course, write about the war."

"Your experiences?"

"Not exactly. But something like that. A wounded man, a hospital, a nurse. But more like . . . well, like a commentary on it. Why war is hell—oh, excuse me."

Her musical laughter made him smile, and she liked to see him smile. "You should hear the language they use in Hollywood. Even on the movie sets. Even while they're shooting scenes, supposedly talking to each other."

The young man looked into her eyes, and she felt the warmth there. He said, "You're a motion-picture star. You have it all. What are you looking for in Paris?"

She frowned, thinking of her confusion about William Desmond Taylor, and shook her head without realizing it. No, she could not go into that with him, not yet. "Oh, just to get away between pictures. My mother"—she glanced through the glass wall of the bar into the hotel lobby and relaxed, seeing her mother was engaged in deep conversation with the wealthy Englishman, Fitch, and would be busy for a while—"my mother thought it a good idea."

"How long will you be here?"

"Until at least New Year's. We have to stay." She bit her lip at the last words, and knew he'd ask her why. She told him as much as she comfortably could about the death of the writer at the party a week earlier, and how the police had instructed them to stay on, how her mother resented the control. "But I wanted to be here on New Year's Eve, anyway."

"A murder! And I saw sort of a ghost last night." As he relayed the encounter to her, Mary's eyes widened. He finished with, "The whole thing sounds like a movie itself. Or a novel."

"That's what I thought. I didn't know him, but to be with him at the party and then find out he's dead an hour later . . . It was awful. Nothing like that has ever happened to me. The ghost can't be real, but everything else is just too real here—a murder, the war, those wounds you got. Your poor legs."

Ernest Hemingway laughed lightly and took Mary

Miles Minter's hand in his. "I'll get over that. My legs will heal. In fact, I want to get into this murder thing while I'm here, as a journalist, you know—what I did before the war. What an opportunity for an article to bring back to the states! I'm going to see that Darnell fellow." He paused. "But reality? Remember, we're real, too. You and me. You're not just a flickering image on a big screen. You're right here, and I can touch you, and that's the kind of reality that's important. And I'm a man, a writer I hope—not just a moving-picture character. That's what we want to take back with us when we leave Paris."

She scowled. "Take back. And lead our separate lives? Me in Hollywood, and you coming back to Paris? Maybe this is all a dream."

"It may be a dream, but right now we're living it, and it's good. We're here together. So let's enjoy our time together. Let's enjoy Paris."

Edda Van Eych felt the warmth of Ricardo Camilo, sitting close to her in the restaurant booth, and wondered whether she was beginning to make another emotional mistake. *I must stay cool and calm, and keep control*, she told herself. She knew she had already lost control of her feelings in a different way with Martin Prince when she met with him, the cruel way he rejected her book. And her attraction to Ricardo at the party, he offering her some comfort and consolation. Now this clandestine meeting at a restaurant a mile from the hotel. She looked furtively about the room, but saw no one she knew.

"Your mind is not here with me, Edda."

She met his eyes. "It is, yes. I am here, Ricardo. I just worry. All of these things at once. My life turns upside down."

"Martin Prince is no prince. More like a devil. He could ruin my career. We share the same view of him, yes?"

She scowled. "Me, he turned down. My book wouldn't be worth the paper it would take to print it on, he said. Insults. Do I deserve it?"

"No. And why does he call us here to tell us?"

"Maybe he just likes to inflict punishment."

Camilo frowned. "There's something even more important. These French police, they talk to me as if I'm a criminal. The death of Thorndyke by the garrote. Yes, Spain invented it, for capital punishment. Now others use it for murder. And I am suspected, just because I come from Spain."

She shivered. "It's a gruesome weapon. Have you seen one?"

"Tell no one—I have one at home. But talk about us, Edda."

"I—I don't know how to say what I feel. My brain tells me one thing, my heart another."

"We have something in common."

"In common? A woman from Holland, a man from Spain? Maybe just that our books were rejected by the same editor." She laughed, knowing the sound came from her lips bitterly.

He shook his head. "The world is changing. The old walls will come down. The war has changed many things." He took her hand in his. "And we are here now, in Paris. Strangers in a strange land, both of us. Paris, the home of love and romance. Let us be part of that."

"Like a shipboard romance. You have a smooth

tongue, but when the boat docks, the lovers go their own ways. It is over."

"No, listen—come to Barcelona with me after all this is over. On the sea there, that is the place for love. A place to forget the war." He reached over and pressed his lips on hers.

Edda Van Eych felt whatever coolness she had retained melt away. *Barcelona!* A place to hide from the world. But she could not commit now. Perhaps when the *Sûreté* said they could leave, when she had true freedom again, then she could decide. For now—abruptly she pushed the thoughts away, and, for this little time, these minutes, she gave in to her emotions.

John Darnell looked quizzically at Inspector Manot. "Mr. and Mrs. Fitch together? I'd prefer a separate inquiry."

Manot frowned. "No. They refused. And without any evidence pointing to anyone, I can only go so far. They are very influential people here." He rapped on their door.

David Fitch opened it with a scowl on his face. "We were expecting you. Damned inconvenience! I hope you won't prolong this." He shook hands with them.

Manot offered apologies as Fitch led the way across the room toward a statuesque woman standing by a sofa. Fitch introduced John Darnell to his wife, Cynthia, who extended her hand to him. Manot nodded at Darnell to begin.

John Darnell took in the height difference in the Fitches, she a good two inches taller with a lithe body, and the age difference, he at least fifty, she in her early thirties. A result of the millions of English pounds the man was reputed to possess? Buying a beautiful wife, as he would an art treasure or a parcel of real estate?

"Why did you come to Paris, Mr. Fitch?" Darnell asked the question of the man but included the wife in his glance. He saw her lips tighten at the question.

"Business. I'm investing in properties here. Now the war's over, things will boom in Paris."

"But to meet with Martin Prince—a New York publisher?"

Fitch waved a hand. "Simple. He has great connections in America. He'll be promoting France in books, through his books and authors. Also, he had some people here from Hollywood." His lips twisted into a proud smirk. "I may buy up a couple of studios."

"Or actresses," his wife put in.

Fitch turned to her. "Please, dear, not now."

Darnell went on. "You talked with Eric Thorndyke."

"I spoke to him at the party. He had a proposition for me."

"I understand you had several meetings with him prior to that party. The purpose?"

"All right. He wanted me to finance a motion picture. A typical thing for the Hollywood types. Looking for a rich mark."

"You refused? Declined the opportunity?"

"Precisely. It did not set too well with him."

"You had words?"

"Words? Look here, I won't stand for that. Who said we argued? It was nothing."

Fitch's wife seemed to be examining her shoes. Her eyes avoided Darnell's. He should question her now.

"Mrs. Fitch—if you don't mind—what was your

impression of Mr. Thorndyke? I suppose you spoke with him on occasion."

She tossed her long blond hair from one side to another as she shook her head, and said, "Not much. Courteous talk at the party, don't you know? He was selling something. But my husband handles that kind of thing, all the business."

"You enjoy Paris?"

"I hadn't visited it for over five years. I was curious."

"Do either of you know any reason for Mr. Thorndyke's murder?"

Their heads shook in unison, and Fitch answered. "He comes from a strange place, this Hollywood, even though he lived in London for some time. There's much under the surface in the film town—partying, drinking, drugs. I'm surprised headlines aren't filled with reports of scandal and murder."

"And the others? Those Prince invited for this soirée? Anyone who met with Prince or attended his party?"

"They don't love each other. But as to a motive for murder, that's one of your specialties, I understand, and Inspector Manot's profession."

"And the ghost? Thorndyke's ghost? Any comments?"

Fitch stood. "Balderdash. I haven't seen it, and I don't believe it. But I can tell you this much—when I see a ghost walking these hotel corridors, that's the day Cynthia and I return to London. And if anyone here wants to question me after that, they can bloody well write my solicitors." He glared at Manot, then at Darnell. "Well, are we done?"

Chapter Six

Penny let herself into their room and called, "John?" As she deposited her handbag on a table, she picked up a glossy announcement lying there. *Adrian!* the sheet proclaimed in French and English. *Master magician performs in the rooftop showroom. 8:30 P.M. and 10:00 P.M. Only six more nights, through New Year's Eve and New Year's Day.* A photograph of a man in a tuxedo smiled out from the page. He held a top hat upside down, and doves seemed to appear from it.

A key rattled in the door, and John Darnell entered. "Have you waited long?" He walked to Penny and took her in his arms. They kissed softly for a moment. "How was Paris, my adventurous wife? And what are you holding there?"

"First, Paris is wonderful. Second, dear, this is our evening's entertainment." She handed him the showroom piece. "I met an interesting woman. She lives in Paris, but she was here at the party that night, saw the murdered man's body. She took me to the Louvre. I saw the Mona Lisa, and John—you never forget the first time you see her."

"Was it her eyes, or the smile?"

"Both. And the hands. But her smile, the most."

"That woman—she saw the dead man?"

"Yes. Her name's Sylvia Beach. She should be on your list. They all had a glimpse of the body."

"Ye-es. Sounds familiar." Darnell glanced over the showroom sheet. "A magician. Just what we need for this case."

She looked at him. "Not going too well?"

He tossed his coat on the bed. "I need to wash off some of the lies these people are laying on me."

"Lies?" She smiled. "How unusual."

He frowned. "I would expect it from one or two. But they're all covering up something. Each one, I suspect, something different. There's a closetful of lies here, mixed with the truth. Mostly, it's what they don't tell me."

"And they're all lying?" She watched as he began washing his hands and face in the bathroom.

He came out, toweling off. "Lies of omission or commission. After I've met all of them, maybe I can piece it together."

Penny freshened herself and changed her wrap. "I'll be going out again after lunch. Are we eating at Armand's?"

"It'll save time."

"Good. My friend will be there. I'll introduce you to her. And then you can make reservations for that show tonight."

"I have to justify why we should look for entertainment. This case is dead serious. It's my job to concentrate on it."

"He's a magician, remember? And you said you needed one."

*   *   *

Ricardo Camilo sat at a small table against the far wall in Armand's restaurant. He muttered, "This table is the worst in the room."

Edda Van Eych, sitting opposite from him, murmured, "Be pleased not to be in the spotlight. You're getting too much attention already."

Camilo looked across the room at John and Penny Darnell as they took seats at a table overlooking the boulevard. "Another troublemaker, there," he said. "The hotel brought him here. He and Manot are thick."

"He's an investigator. Just stay away from him."

"So he will talk with me. Another interrogation."

"Keep your mouth shut tight. Say as little as possible, volunteer nothing, don't get drunk, and you may stay out of trouble."

They buried their faces in the large menus and studied the selections. Camilo knew appearances of normalcy were important at this point. Dining in public. Talking casually. Making some pretense. To keep suspicion away.

As Darnell and Penny took seats, a small woman with bobbed hair walked over to them from a nearby table, where she had been sitting alone.

Penny said, "John, this is Sylvia Beach."

Darnell stood and took the slim hand the woman held out. "Sit with us for a while. Penny told me of your adventures."

"If you can call museums adventures." She laughed.

Darnell spoke seriously. "If you don't mind—you know I'm investigating circumstances surrounding the death of Eric Thorndyke."

"Yes." She looked at Penny.

"Did you know him at all before he came to Paris? And—well, I'd appreciate hearing whatever else you can tell me about that night."

"I didn't know anyone here. I'd written to Martin Prince. I talked with him about the bookshop I want to open, to ask whether I could get his firm's books. He was very encouraging. I told him I might want to sponsor some writers, if I could."

"Help them get published?"

"Perhaps. Not now, of course. Later on."

"And Thorndyke?"

"We didn't talk much. He was more interested in others."

"Who?"

Sylvia Beach stared at the white tablecloth, finally looking up and saying, "The Dutch woman. Prince's associate, Patricia. Mrs. Fitch. The young actress. All the women there, I think."

"Business?"

She smiled at that. "His kind of business, I suppose." She stood. "I can't tell you much more. But later, if you have questions, let me know. I'll leave you now. See you after lunch, Penny?"

"Yes, and we're going to the magic show tonight. Will you come?"

Sylvia nodded vigorously. "I need a change. I'll be there."

Darnell shook his head. "Curiouser and curiouser."

"Not so curious. Thorndyke was simply a ladies' man."

"Perhaps."

*   *   *

After lunch, Penny said, "I'll see you later." She left Darnell and walked to the table where Sylvia Beach sat alone.

Darnell checked the time. In fifteen minutes he was due at Bardon's office to join Manot for the afternoon schedule.

He stopped at the reception desk and reserved seats for the 8:30 P.M. performance of Adrian the Magician. As he stood there, a man approached him.

"Professor Darnell? I'm Bert Ward. I'm your five p.m. appointment."

Darnell waited, knowing more was coming. He studied the stocky, heavy man. Three-piece plaid suit, flower in the lapel, a watch chain crisscrossing his vest, a professional-looking camera on a cord about his neck. At length, he said, "Yes?"

"We could talk now, perhaps down in the lobby."

"All right, although the Inspector should be in on any interviews," Darnell said.

They walked to the curved staircase and down to the busy Le Grand lobby. The man led the way to a table in a corner. As they took seats, he handed Darnell a business card.

Darnell looked at the words on the card: BERT WARD. BODYGUARD, with a London address and phone number.

"Bodyguard for the Fitches. We thought as much."

"I'm their aide also. Carry suitcases, go here, go there."

"Nothing you say surprises me. Are you concerned with your clients' safety? Is that it?"

"Thorndyke's murder changed everything. I have to watch my step, protect them and myself."

"Do you know anything about Thorndyke's murder? Do you think there might be another murder? That someone might attack Mr. or Mrs. Fitch?"

"I don't know who to suspect or what to think. This is out of my realm. I wanted to ask you if you've found out anything. I have to admit the ghost thing does bother me."

"The ghost thing—you saw it?"

"Yes, I'm quite sure I did. I was coming back up from the brasserie one night, after a few pints of ale. Got off the elevator, and there he was down at the end of the hall by Prince's suite. I had my camera on, but I knew I didn't have time to take a photo— it's pretty complicated. But while I hesitated, he disappeared."

"Literally? In thin air?"

"There was a little puff of smoke and he was gone."

"Thank you for telling me. I can't give you any advice. The Fitches will have to stay here as long as the Inspector can keep them. So just be alert. If anything happens that makes you think your clients are in danger, let me or the Inspector know at once."

"I just don't like being involved in a murder case. I have to watch my back."

"I'll tell the Inspector what you said, and your concerns. I'd suggest you talk with him yourself. Otherwise, continue on your job. Don't involve yourself in the Thorndyke case."

Darnell stood. "Mr. Ward, we'll consider our appointment for today concluded unless the Inspector wants to meet with you. No need to wait for us at five."

Ward stood and glanced at the bar. "If you need me later, check the brasserie. I like to take a few pints at night."

Upon reaching Bardon's office and joining up with
Manot for their next appointment, Darnell passed on
the information Ward had given him. They walked
down the corridor toward the elevators.

Manot smiled. "He sounds scared, for a bodyguard."

"I think there's more he's not telling us. He was
trying to get information, not give it. But it was interesting to talk to another witness to the ghost. People
aren't imagining it."

Darnell noticed a brass plate on one of the mezzanine doors: PAUL PASCAL, *DOCTEUR*, LE GRAND HOTEL,
and stopped at the door.

"Is he available? I'd like to speak with him."

Manot nodded. "*Mais oui*. He should be in."

The Inspector entered the office, followed by Darnell. A young woman at a desk looked up and said,
"Inspector Manot."

"This is Professor Darnell. We'd like to see the
doctor."

She glanced at a calendar pad. "He has no appointments for an hour. I'll ring him." She picked up a
connecting phone, spoke into it, then hung it up. "Go
right in."

In the inner office, they found Dr. Pascal just rising
from his chair to greet them. After introductions,
Darnell said, "It's about the death of Eric Thorndyke."

"*Certainement*. How may I assist?"

"Just one or two questions. Have you ever seen a
death by this method before?"

"By garrote? Never. But the wounds were unmis-
takable."

"I suppose that method would require great strength?"

Dr. Pascal nodded. *"Très difficile.* The instrument is deadly, but it would require a person somewhat strong with steady nerves. A cold, hard person. The victim would struggle violently, and cry out. Of course, M'sieur Thorndyke was drunk."

"The important question I have, after hearing that, is whether a woman could have done it. There were a number of women at that party."

Dr. Pascal sighed. "A strong woman, a coldhearted one, perhaps. It's not impossible. But my only definite statement is that one person, whether man or woman, used a thin wire or cord to kill the man, and death was by suffocation." He spread his hands wide. "That is all I can really say with certainty."

As they walked on to the elevators, Darnell said, "So, we can't eliminate the women as suspects. Could be a man or woman. You found nothing at the scene pointing to one or the other?" He smiled. "No single cuff link, no earring torn off in a struggle?"

Manot laughed. "A convenient piece of evidence like that would make it easy, would it not?"

"The son discovered the father. How long was he alone with him after he determined he was dead?"

"He said others swarmed around immediately."

"When he went into the bedroom, did he close the door behind him?"

Manot shrugged. "No one has commented. Probably no one noticed." He looked at Darnell. "You are thinking . . . ?"

"Nothing. Just asking."

Manot knocked on the door to room 908, and in minutes the two men faced Brandon Tyler, who took a seat opposite them in a straight-backed chair.

"Back problems," Tyler said. "I must sit on a firm chair. You were saying . . . ?"

Darnell answered. "We were asking—did you work out your publishing arrangements with Martin Prince?"

"I thought this meeting was about Eric Thorndyke."

"All right, then, we'll come back to the publishing. You knew Eric Thorndyke?"

"I met him once in London, but the paths of those from Hollywood don't cross mine that often. It was some years ago. A different world, then."

"Yes, but the same man. The subject then?"

"He wrote novels at that time. We talked casually. We had no business dealings. It was a small social gathering."

"Where?"

"A party at the Fitches'. They were quite social, and he was always looking for business deals."

"You and Thorndyke both came here . . . A coincidence?"

"Martin Prince invited me, but it was more of demand, really. I publish his books in London." He scowled. "At least I have been doing that. He wanted to talk."

"You will continue, then? You settled all that with him?"

"I don't know. He didn't say much, said he hadn't made a final decision. I think he might be shopping around."

"And there are other London firms that do exactly what yours does?"

"Unfortunately, yes. And some of them for less money."

Darnell eyed the Spaniard who sat across the table from himself and Manot. Olive complexion. A surly, or suspicious look. Under pressure because of the use of the Spanish garrote. Not a friendly witness by any means.

"Have you seen the hotel ghost?" Darnell asked. "Do you know anything about it?"

"Nothing."

"You're writing a book."

"It's about an uprising in Spain."

"That sounds like a dangerous political subject."

Camilo nodded. "Prince said that, too. I write of cannons and machine guns, exciting battles, the capture of Madrid, and a new governmnent. He said it was not—what was his word—realistic?"

"And Thorndyke? Did you have any dealings with him?"

"When Prince turned me down, I spoke to the senior Thorndyke, who was planning to return to Hollywood. I thought he could develop a good motion picture of my book, with all the action in it." He shook his head. "But he declined."

"The night of the killing . . . what can you tell me, what did you observe? Especially regarding Thorndyke."

"He was having a good time." Camilo smiled. "Talking with the ladies. His son—well, he did not seem to like that. I saw him looking at his father, frowning."

"Did you see the son enter the bedroom where

his father had retired, just before Thorndyke's body was discovered?"

Camilo took a breath and spoke hesitantly. "I saw him enter. The door closed. I looked away, then someone brought me a drink. The door opened again and he shouted to us, and we all gathered at the doorway. I looked in. The man was dead."

Manot and Darnell exchanged glances. Darnell asked in a casual tone, "And how long was he in there with his father?"

His forehead creased. "Not long. A few minutes. I was speaking to someone. Had no reason to notice that."

Manot said, "Professor Darnell is interested in anything you can tell him about the garrote."

"I knew you would bring that up again—I'm Spanish, and so they suspect me." He paused. "The garrote is an ancient instrument. It was invented three hundred years ago, and at first just used for executions. That is all I know."

"You have seen one before?"

"Only in museums. Such weapons are not for ordinary citizens."

Darnell stood. "Nor do ordinary writers find their death in that way, nor do ghosts ordinarily parade about hotel corridors at midnight. No, Señor Camilo, nothing at all about this case is ordinary."

Chapter Seven

Darnell and Inspector Manot stood outside the door of Edda Van Eych's room. "Two more appointments before five p.m.," Manot said, making notes on his list. "The Dutch woman and the girl from Hollywood with her mother."

In moments, Edda Van Eych opened the door in response to Manot's knock, and the two men sat facing her. After introductions, Darnell said, "You seem to have more than one distinction in this matter, madame. You not only associated with Eric Thorndyke at the party, but you claim to have seen his ghost."

"I claim? You doubt it? Yes, it vas him, I have no doubts . . . but I do not believe in spirits or ghosts. I only know what I saw."

"And describe that, please."

She stared at a point on the wall behind Darnell's head. "It was about midnight. I had come from— spending time with friends. I opened my door, heard something, turned and looked down the hallway. He stood there, looking just like he did at the party. The same black evening clothes, the same red tie and red waist device. Very distinctive. And then he was gone."

"In a puff of smoke?"

She looked at Darnell. "Yes, but—"

He waved a hand. "You spent time with him at the party. You knew his looks, his features. There could be no mistake?"

She shook her head. "I saw what I saw. At the party—well, yes, we talked. He needed someone to listen to him and to his complaints. But he did not quite reveal the true nature of them. I just know some of it involved Prince. No surprise at that. I had my own problems with him."

"Did he say anything to you to give you any idea as to a motive for his murder?"

She frowned and brushed back strands of dark hair from her forehead. "He said something about a special project. But he told me nothing more. Acted mysterious about it, even after he drank so much. The champagne didn't loosen his tongue, but he did get a fierce headache. You know the rest."

Charlotte Shelby refilled her champagne flute from the bottle on the glass table and watched her daughter flip idly through a magazine on the sofa. Charlotte wanted to gather her thoughts carefully before she presented them. Dealing with a sixteen-year-old girl, even one who had starred in over two dozen movies, was at best difficult, and more often now, impossible.

She decided on an indirect approach. "Tell me about your soldier friend," she invited.

Mary Miles Minter looked up and tossed her magazine aside. Charlotte saw a glow spread across her daughter's face.

"He's really nice, Mother. He was wounded in the

war. Wants to be a writer. Was one, for a newspaper."

"What did you talk about?"

"Oh . . . Hollywood. I told him to come there. They need writers for lots of things, but . . ." Mary's face clouded.

"Yes, dear?" Charlotte was pleased Mary had found a friend to take her mind off William Desmond Taylor. But now she began to worry about this new man—young, no money, probably no future.

"He said he was going to come back here to Paris. He wants to study writing here. Loves writing and wants to write poems, stories, a novel. Says Paris will be like a 'Mecca for writers'—whatever that means."

"It means, dear, they'll come here and carouse around with each other, drink in bars, go to the Folies Bergere . . ." She caught herself in her diatribe, realizing that the man planned to come back to Paris, out of reach of her daughter. She added quickly, "But it is a great place for writers. Very inspirational."

Mary's laugh bore a bitter tinge. "Mother, you're as transparent as a window glass. I don't know why I tell you anything." She picked up the magazine again and held it in front of her face.

Charlotte fidgeted. "That professor is due any minute. Just remember, don't volunteer information. And don't mention Taylor. There are plenty of rumors out there already."

"Oh, Mother!"

The rap on the door ended what might have gone on to become one of their usual unresolved disagreements. Charlotte Shelby tugged down her dress, straightening it, as she walked to the door. She opened it to the two men.

*   *   *

Looking at Mary Miles Minter and her mother, side by side, John Darnell felt the contrast in spirit between them, but he also saw their close resemblance. In her prime, Charlotte Shelby no doubt charmed legions of men, as her daughter did now each night on the screen.

"We appreciate your seeing us, Mrs. Shelby," he said.

"This has been very inconvenient, forcing us to stay here like common criminals." She looked from Manot to Darnell.

"Mother, it's *Paris*," Mary said. "I don't mind. And we'll be in Paris on New Year's Eve!"

"Mary—"

Darnell rushed on, "Mrs. Shelby—and Miss Minter—think back to the night of the party, if you can put yourself there."

Charlotte rubbed one arm with her other hand. "There was no ghost that night. The Thorndyke man was alive, very much alive."

"Did he bother you?"

"I had to watch him every minute." She looked at her daughter. "He had an eye for women. Yes, he did."

"He, ah, approached your daughter?"

"Touched her, patted her. I had to come between them. Then he tried his charm on me." She sniffed. "Tacky. We'd call him tacky in Looz-iana."

Darnell nodded. "Did anyone quarrel with him?"

"He drank a lot. There were some loud words here and there, but, of course, everyone was loud. Too loud."

"Tacky?"

Charlotte Shelby smiled. "Yes, I'd call it that."

Darnell turned to Mary. "Does this seem like a bad motion picture to you, Miss Minter?"

Mary Minter shivered. "I'm starting to dream about it. The body. Soldiers hobbling about, some of them with missing limbs. It's too real. I'm used to a make-believe world."

"Did the elder Mr. Thorndyke's attentions bother you?"

She shook her head, her curls bobbing back and forth. "No. Even if it's Paris, he just acted like all men. They think girls, and women, are playthings. When I began in pictures, I thought there were some real gentlemen in the movie business—a few, at least." She sighed and looked away. "But even with the best ones, you never know for sure."

After a few more questions they left the actress and her mother. Darnell and Manot rode the elevator down to the main floor, walked into the lobby and took two chairs out of the flow of movement.

Manot challenged him. "So do you have any conclusions?"

"Inspector, I know my assignment here for the hotel only deals with the sightings, but I think both things are inevitably tied together—the ghost and the murder. Let's talk about the ghost. Two of Martin Prince's entourage have seen the ghost, Edda Van Eych and Bert Ward. Last night, the young soldier saw him. Who were the others?"

"Here's the entire list. The first time it was two guests, a woman and a man staying in 901, near the Thorndyke suite. They told me their story, and checked out. Also, a single woman saw it, and she has also left the hotel. Then the Dutch woman, on Christmas Eve. Ward, as you said. A group coming from a party left the elevator on the wrong floor, and while they were waiting for another elevator, saw it down the hall. Then last night, your soldier. And two of our maids reported seeing it from a distance. One saw it clearly. Descriptions all consistent."

"The maids are still here?"

Manot nodded. "You may speak with them, naturally."

Darnell said, "There is no ghost, as such, of course, although whoever it was looked real to those who saw him."

"What they saw, your ghost, will lead us to the murderer?"

"Unless you get there first, Inspector."

Manot sighed. "What else would you have me do for you?"

"Are the maids still here at this hour? Let's get Bardon, and all go to see them. I have some questions."

When they picked Bardon up from his office, he said, "Their station is on the ninth floor. They cover eight, nine, and ten."

They took the elevator up to the ninth floor, and Bardon led the way to a room the size of a small bedroom in which shelves bore loads of sheets and towels, tablecloths, soaps, and cleaning supplies. As they entered, the lone occupant, a very slender, flat-bodied woman in a white uniform, turned toward them.

"*Bonjour, Directeur.*" She made a little curtsy. Her eyes widened as she gave a worried look to the men.

"They speak very little English," Bardon said to Darnell. "I'll have to interpret for you."

"Of course. Is she the one who saw the, ah, ghost?"

"Yes, and another was with her."

"Perhaps she could find the other and bring her back. Tell her it is just to ask some questions for a few minutes."

Bardon transmitted the request in French and the maid left. In five minutes she returned with a second, taller, heavier maid in a similar white uniform and with a shock of bright red hair.

Bardon asked them to take seats in the two chairs by a table, and the men stood opposite them. "Proceed," Bardon said.

"Ask first, when did they see the ghost, and second, to describe the thing to me. One maid at at time."

In French, Bardon addressed the wiry maid he called Claire. When he stopped speaking, the woman nodded, took a deep breath, and began speaking to him in a rapid flow of French that quickly lost Darnell, despite his previous studies of the language.

Bardon translated: " 'I was on the floor late that night'—she says—'behind in my work in the storage room here, preparing linens for the next day. I'd finished what was needed on ten, and was on nine. I had one more floor to go, eight, after that.' "

Bardon spoke to her in French again, Darnell understanding his words to mean, "Please continue."

The woman glanced at her maid companion, who nodded.

The first maid went on expressively, gesturing, her eyes first widening and then narrowing with the story, staring first at Manot, then Bardon, then Darnell. At last she stopped, with a nervous smile, and looked at Darnell. He smiled at her.

Bardon translated while, as he spoke each word, the maid continued to fix her gaze on Darnell. " 'I left this room and was walking to the stairs to go down to the eighth floor'—the maid says—'when I saw him. *Mon Dieu!*' she says. 'He was in evening clothes and had a strange expression on his face, which was very white. I dropped the cloths I was carrying and ran back to this room. Rosette was here.' " Bardon paused, looking at him.

Darnell nodded. "Go on, then."

"She said she found Rosette, and the two of them went back out into the hall, but he was gone."

"So the second maid, Rosette, actually saw nothing?"

Bardon asked a quick question of the larger woman, then replied. "It would seem that is so."

"Ask Claire three more things for me. Exactly what was he wearing, how close was she to him, and did she recognize him?"

Bardon translated, obtained a reply, asked one more thing, and gave her answer. "A tuxedo, evening clothes, a red bow tie, a dozen or more feet away." He spoke a few more words.

"Did she recognize him?

"No, not at all. But I asked her about the cummerbund, and she remembered that."

"Then one last thing," Darnell said, and looked at Claire as he posed the question. "Could she identify him if she ever saw him again?"

The woman shrank back and put her hand to her mouth. "No, m'sieur! No!"

Bardon spoke rapidly to her, then to Darnell. "She knew enough English to be scared by your question, but got it wrong. She thought you were going to bring the ghost to her."

Darnell offered a wry smile to the woman, saying partly in French, partly English, "If you understand me, Claire, do not worry—there is no ghost." To Bardon, he said, "Reassure her, Jacques."

Jacques Bardon said some comforting words at length in French, and the three men left the maids to talk with each other.

After they left the room and were out of earshot, Darnell said, "No, I will not bring a ghost to her. That is the truth. But I may have to ask her to identify a man who pretends to be one."

Manot said, "Tomorrow morning, we'll meet with Mr. Bardon's Chairman, and my Chief Inspector, in the director's office. They'll be eager to hear from you. Each day we draw farther away from the crime."

"But not from the criminal, Inspector. Among those twelve guests, we still have a killer walking the halls of this hotel. And whoever it is, is more dangerous than the ninth-floor ghost."

Philip Thorndyke sat at the edge of the sofa glaring at a cross-legged Edda Van Eych, who relaxed in an easy chair opposite him. "This wasn't a good idea. I don't know why you're here."

"Now, Philip. You really do know, don't you? We have things we can do for each other."

"Such as?"

She shook her head. "It's your father's secret I want. And I can keep yours."

"My secret?"

"What happened in your father's room when you went in there, the night of the party."

His voice betrayed no emotion. "I found him dead."

"I notice things. I remember things. Your father was rich. He had this valuable work, his secret. It's all yours now. You stayed in there with the door closed for several minutes before you opened it. Long enough for you to . . . Must I say it?"

"To murder my own father? Have you told this nonsense to others? You could get into serious trouble spreading lies."

"I'll forget all that. Frankly, I don't care. It's that secret work that Eric finished . . . Give that to me and I keep what I know just between us."

"You know nothing, damn you! I'll ask you to leave now."

She stood, moving closer to him. "That Professor is just getting started on his inquiries, Philip. Who knows what secrets he'll uncover?" She touched his cheek. "I know you have your father's work. Bring it to me. We can help each other."

Chapter Eight

Friday afternoon, December 27

Brandon Tyler rapped loudly on Martin Prince's door, and when Prince opened it, walked in past him without an invitation. "I've got some things to say to you," he said, his voice filled with emotion.

Prince shook his head in seeming wonder, closed the door, and returned to his seat on the sofa where he had been nursing a glass of champagne. An open bottle and several glasses stood on a tray on the table. He looked at Tyler. "All right. Sit down. Get yourself a glass of bubbly. I know what's on your mind."

"Damn right you do." Tyler glared at him, but shortly filled a glass to the point of overflowing and took a large swallow. "I've been thinking about what you said at the party last week—and what you didn't say. And I'm about to boil over."

Although Prince offered a stiff smile, his eyes were cold. "Go on."

"You as much as said you were going to get a new publishing outlet in London. I don't like dangling on the end of a rope."

Prince nodded. "Yes, I hinted I'd be looking around a bit. The war's over, and we need an aggressive correspondent company in London, for all England. The stakes are pretty high."

Tyler finished his drink and slammed the glass down on the table. "I've been attached to American-Universal for fifteen years—before you were even there. If the Chairman hadn't died . . ."

Prince smiled without humor. "But he did. And some of the old ways died with him. We're in the twentieth century now. Time we faced that."

"You can't just ditch me. I'll complain to—to the highest people in New York."

Prince looked down into his glass. "They know my mission here. They also know what the stakes are. And they expect me to perform. Believe me."

Tyler stood. "I can't believe anything you say. Just be careful, Martin. Be very careful." He turned on his heel and took long strides to the door, which he opened and slammed behind him as he left.

Martin Prince refilled his champagne glass and walked over to the window. He stared out at the distant profile of the Eiffel Tower and took a thoughtful sip. At the sound of a light rap on his door, he turned to see Patricia August enter. She closed the door, leaned back against it, and said, "I heard that. These walls aren't soundproof and our balcony doors were open."

"Come in. I could use a little company just now. This looks like one of those bad days. If Tyler knew what I have to go through—well, maybe he wouldn't · complain so much."

"He sounded very angry, even dangerous."

"Bluster. He'll calm down. He'll have to face reality. We all have to do that."

* * *

Edda Van Eych stared above the rim of her glass of red wine at Ricardo Camilo across from her at the table in his room. Camilo filled his own glass and tossed the now-empty bottle into a nearby trash basket.

She said, "You shouldn't have lied." She watched Camilo's eyes. She had discovered that whenever Camilo lied his eyes narrowed into slits.

Camilo laughed. "I didn't lie to them. I merely said nothing about it."

"In court, when they want the truth, they ask for the whole truth and nothing but the truth."

Camilo looked unsmiling at her now. "What exactly do you object to? What would you have had me do?"

"All I know is that you told me you had a garrote. You tell them you only saw one in a museum? Ha!"

Camilo said in a soft voice, "Let us call it my own private museum. And I did not bring it with me to Paris."

"You say."

"Yes, I say." He glared at her. "And what are you going to do about it? Run to the Inspector? Turn me in for not divulging that bit of information? I never denied seeing one."

"I don't like it."

"Look, Edda, this will be over soon and I'll go back to Spain, to Barcelona. You can go with me. We can survive. The Professor asks questions, the Inspector worries, the Manager frets—but nothing happens. They have no evidence."

"They don't, yet," she said. "But there's something in the air, vibrations. I can feel these things, just like my old Dutch grandmother, Johanna, could sense things. She even predicted the exact day she was to die. Cried about dying for weeks ahead."

"And what do you predict?"

"Trouble. For you and for me." She swallowed the last of her wine. "Just be careful."

He took her in his arms. "I will. Like your *abuela*, Johanna, there's two things I don't like. Trouble and death."

Mary Miles Minter stared at her mother after the Inspector and Professor Darnell left their room. She could sense Charlotte Shelby had something on her mind, and knew she'd get no peace until she addressed it. She tossed her magazine down and said, "All right, Mother. Tell me what it is. I can't stand to see you fidgeting and pacing around the room straightening pictures and all that. What is bothering you?"

"These talks with the investigators, they're stirring up things. I'm remembering things about the party, about what you did there."

"And what did I do? I behaved myself like a young lady—that's what you said to do, didn't you? Don't you always say, be a young lady, as if I'd go on a rampage if you didn't?"

"You know the trouble with William Desmond Taylor."

"He's gone, Mother. He went into the Canadian army. I may never see him again."

"He'll direct you in your new films."

"So? You don't want the million-dollar contract? Fifty thousand a picture, right? You can buy a lot of Japanese silk stockings for that." She sniffed, and primped her hair with both hands, waiting. She knew her mother would come to the point soon.

"You heard something at the party. Someone told you something, and I think it was the dead man."

"Dead men don't talk."

"Earlier, Juliet."

Mary looked at her. "You haven't called me Juliet in a long time."

"It's always in my mind. Your real name still means a lot to me. It was almost like your grandmother's name—Julia—and you were her favorite."

"All right, Mother."

"So what did Eric Thorndyke say to you? He was hovering around you, pawing you, whispering in your ear. I saw."

"He did that to all the women. I saw all that, too."

Charlotte Shelby's eyes flashed. "Come out with it. He told you about a script, didn't he? I heard that word, too."

Mary breathed deeply and let it out. "I didn't want to tell you, I know how you are, how you'd get all excited."

"Tell me, Mary!"

Mary spread both arms in the air. "Yes, there was a special movie script of some kind. It had a part for a young woman in it. Sort of a love triangle. He said I'd be perfect in the part." She laughed. "But he was good at lying. I think he would have promised me the moon that night if . . ."

"If what?"

"Oh, never mind."

Charlotte thought for a moment. She rose and paced back and forth across the room, then stopped and glared at Mary. "I've got to have that script. Did he tell you where it is?"

"I don't know. Maybe in his room. Maybe Philip has it. Wouldn't the son get what the father had? Just don't make a big scene, Mother. I know how you get when you smell money."

* * *

Patricia August answered the knock on her door with some anticipation and anxiety. It was him; she knew it by the way he knocked—two raps, a pause, and a third. Opening the door, she saw him standing there, smiling, and she pulled him into her room, at the same time glancing up and down the empty ninth-floor corridor.

"You shouldn't have come," she said, but didn't mean it.

"I had to. Do you know how long it's been?"

"Before our one stolen hour last week—almost two years. I hope it won't be two years again."

David Fitch shook his head. "Never. I'm going to give Cynthia that divorce I know she wants, but I'm not going to pay her a fortune. She could never get one. She has no evidence."

"You have to be careful."

"I have been. I don't think she suspects a thing. She's so busy with her own peccadilloes."

Trisha smiled. "Cynthia is involved with another man? Really?"

"That's a polite way of putting it. I'm not sure who it is. I just know it's someone."

Trisha pulled away from him and faced the window. "By the way she makes love to you?"

He grabbed her shoulders and pulled her back into his arms. "By the way she *doesn't*. We haven't as much as kissed in months."

Trisha turned her face to his. When the kiss ended, she sighed. "I can't believe it's going to happen. After years of waiting." She peered into his eyes. "Do you remember? Do you remember our first time?"

"I'll never forget it. I want to go there again, to that little hotel overlooking the Pacific Ocean. Maybe we could even get the same room."

She smiled. "You *are* sentimental, aren't you? The big businessman—with a heart."

"A heart for you." He looked at his watch. "I'm going to see your boss in about an hour. I've got some things to say to him he won't like."

"Martin said he was expecting a bad day. Now I know why." She kissed him again, more passionately this time. "But let's not talk about business. Let's treasure every minute."

He pressed his lips on hers, and she loosened his tie.

Charlotte Shelby knocked on Philip Thorndyke's door. She had heard he seldom left his room. How he could mope in there and brood about his father's murder, she could not imagine. A possible answer flashed in her mind. Maybe it was pretense. There seemed to be no love lost between Philip and Eric Thorndyke. They didn't seem close at the party. After some moments, she wondered if he was in the room, and knocked again.

The door opened abruptly, and a sleepy-eyed Philip looked out at her. "Mrs. Shelby?"

Crisply, she said, "I'd like to see you. On a bit of business."

"Business?"

"May I come in, or shall I stand out here in the hallway for all to see."

He stood aside, and waved her in with his hand. "Be my guest. This hotel is like Grand Central Station in New York. People throw parties, they get drunk, they get murdered here. They ask me for things. And me? I just pay the hotel bill."

She marched past him, ignoring the comments, and took a seat in a straight chair at the table. That would seem most businesslike, she thought. She imagined he would sit opposite her, and he did.

"Now . . ." He rubbed his forehead. "Damn headaches. Can't get rid of them."

"Poor boy." She followed his cue. "You should get out, see something of life."

"You're right . . . but what do you want? You and I haven't talked much. So you're the beautiful actress's mother?"

"Yes, they call me that. Mary Miles Minter's mother. But I also manage her career." She paused. "That's why I'm here."

"Okay."

"I understand your father wrote a script, something special, that featured a young woman. A part that would fit my daughter perfectly."

He raised his eyebrows. "The script, yes. He was secretive about his work, and I don't know what's in it. I don't know anything about a part. How do you know all this?"

"Never mind how I know. The point is, I'm prepared to offer you a good price for the script. Of course, I'll have to read it first."

"It's gone."

Her eyes widened. "What?"

"It hasn't been seen since my father died." He gestured toward the bedroom door.

"You searched for it?"

"I went through his things. I wasn't looking for it,

but I noticed the package wasn't there. He had wrapped and tied it up with string."

Charlotte bit her lip in disappointment, but quickly recovered. It wouldn't do to reveal her strong interest in it to this man, but she had to keep him connected. She stood. "Well, if you do find it, you'll call me, won't you?"

He stood facing her and took the hand she held out to him. "All right, but it's not a high priority for me. My father's murder . . ."

She gave him what she hoped was a sympathetic smile, but her thoughts were on the script and how to get it. She simply said, "Yes, that must be solved."

Philip walked her to the door.

"Thank you, Philip. Take care of yourself."

"It's time that I start to do that."

As he was closing the door behind her he muttered, "I'll start with a little drink."

At exactly five p.m., Martin Prince reluctantly admitted David Fitch to his room. *Another sour apple I have to bite into today*, he thought, as he observed Fitch choose his chair carefully and wait for Prince to be seated before saying a word. He grimaced. First Tyler, now David Fitch. But Fitch seemed not to have as much fervor at the moment as Prince expected from the man's earlier loud-voiced, room-to-room phone call. At the moment, he actually seemed quite relaxed. But he was sure the man would warm to whatever proposal he came to advance. Then a disagreement would result. Fitch's pattern.

"You wanted to see me," Prince said. He decided to act condescending. "How can I help you?"

Fitch colored. "You can help by explaining why you called me an unprincipled raider. I'll have you know I'm an investor. Yes, I'm planning to take an ownership position in your firm. The stock's on the market for all to buy."

"You want thirty percent. With the stock so widely held you'd have the controlling interest. I call that raiding, yes."

Fitch's voice took on an earnest tone. "And why do you object to my ownership, even control? I've done well by companies I control. Their performance and stocks have gone up. I know you own seven percent of American-Universal yourself."

"The stock could dip. Seven percent of nothing is nothing. I don't like the way you chop out management when you take control."

"Look, my man, there's no need for bickering."

Prince's lips tightened. "I'm not your man."

"Speaking of management, I don't know why you don't promote your assistant, Miss August. Isn't she the one there who makes you look good, does all the brain work? Frankly, Prince, I have doubts about your executive ability if you can't see that."

Prince growled. "You're meddling already. Yes, she's competent, but what do you expect—Vice President?"

"Why not? A woman can be very effective. The right woman."

Prince saw the direction of the talk and gave him a wry smile. "You want her promoted."

"I merely suggest it."

"Any other—suggestions?"

"You could pick your prospective writers a bit more carefully. That bloody Dutch woman. And the Spaniard, with his garrotes."

"That's not proven."

"No. But who's listening? The point is, you need some good writers if you're going to take advantage of the groundswell in the twenties. It's going to be a great decade for smart people."

Prince stood. He could feel his face was red now, the way it turned when his anger was about to overflow. He had to end this before that happened. In a restrained voice he said, "If you'll excuse me now, I have things to do. I'll . . . consider your suggestions."

Fitch also stood, and strode to the door. As he left, he turned and said, "Until our next little talk."

When the door closed behind Fitch, Prince expressed his frustration with a single word. "Damn!" He walked to the door leading to his balcony, stepped out, and took a deep breath.

Chapter Nine

In the darkened room on the tenth floor penthouse of Le Grand Hotel, Darnell could feel the tension and excitement of the people at small round tables. He clinked his champagne flute to Penny's water glass. "Here's to magic!"

"You can't really mean that. I'm sure magic has no more credibility for you than ghosts or apparitions."

Darnell smiled. "One must be open, *n'est-ce pas*?"

"Speaking French? After one day here?"

"After four years of study, I could be more fluent with a bit of practice. And when in France, do as the French do."

He idly glanced at Sylvia Beach at her table. "Let's invite your friend to sit with us," he said to Penny.

Penny stepped over to Sylvia's table and brought her back. "Much better," Penny said. "We can talk. And the show's on."

The Master of Ceremonies stepped out onto the stage in a spotlight projected from the top and back of the room. *"Mesdames et messieurs . . .* ladies and gentlemen . . . *votre attention, s'il vous plaît."* The audience settled down.

He went on, "In a moment, I will introduce to you Adrian, the world-famous magician from London." He informed the audience that Adrian would describe his magical presentations in both French and English.

"A chance to practice your French, John," Penny whispered.

To a round of applause a man of average height but obvious great presence and charm stepped out onto the stage with a swirl of his red-lined black cape. He tipped his top hat as he gestured in the air with a sweep of an ornate black and silver wand. A black moustache adorned his upper lip and a perfectly pointed beard jutted out from his chin—but Darnell wondered whether either was real, or simply stock-in-trade for performing magicians, fixed in place with spirit gum.

Adrian's voice resounded. "Ladies and gentlemen— for your mystification and delight, I am pleased to present magic flowing from the darkest reaches of the mind and the farthest reaches of the continents. I bring sights from magicians in Spain and India, and from sorcerers in Beirut and Bucharest, who have passed their secrets on to me."

With a flourish, he produced, seemingly from the air, a bouquet of fresh flowers, and presented them to a woman at a front table to the sound of spirited applause. Quickly he displayed a variety of sleight-of-hand tricks involving his hat, doves, his wand, and colorful silk scarves first tied end to end and the next moment remarkably separated.

After some minutes, he produced from his hat— rather predictably, Darnell felt—a small white rabbit. He handed it to a dazzling, petite young red-haired girl in an abbreviated, bright costume acting as his assistant. This drew exclamations from the women in the audience and applause from the men.

Penny smiled at Darnell and Sylvia. "Are the men applauding the rabbit—or the girl?"

"Men in Paris are appreciative of a neatly turned ankle."

"Ankle, indeed!"

The magician went on from one trick to another, quickly changing costumes twice, building to his finale exactly at the one-hour point. As a finale, he waved his wand at his red-haired assistant, who promptly vanished in a bright flash. In the next minute, he tapped on a large, round box, and she stepped out and bowed, to the delight and the applause of the audience.

"I enjoyed it," Penny said, as they rose and merged with the crowd proceeding to the exits.

"Ye-es. Magical."

"You're looking into magic to solve your case?"

"No. But I do have an idea—thanks to the show."

Adrian Granger—known more familiarly wherever he performed as simply Adrian the Magician—sat before the dressing-room table in the small room adjacent to the stage of Le Grand's showroom. He pulled down the rim of one eye, then the other, looking at the red lines in the whites.

"Damned late nights and smoky rooms," he mumbled, talking to himself as he often did when alone. He glanced at his watch. Twenty minutes until the next hour show—but then the other business. He'd leave the moustache and beard on, but he itched to pull them off and cleanse his face with warm, sudsy water.

"One more bloody year," he said, "and I'm done with all this."

He pulled a bottle of scotch from the dresser drawer and poured a quantity of it into a small water glass. He tossed it off, poured another and stared at it. He hated the lonely life of traveling from city to city, and drank too much when he did.

After an early army discharge due to an injury, he had traveled with his act in England for a year, but now, the war over, he ventured again onto the Continent. Yet the traveling prevented him from becoming more involved in stage shows in London's theater district.

This trip had turned out to be particularly nerve-wracking, and he was not compensated sufficiently, even with the extra money he was being paid. He didn't like what he'd found himself in, and wished for January first, when it would all be over. And yet . . .

Adrian opened a drawer and stared at its contents. He could make something to his advantage from this. Knowing the people, he speculated that a few thousand pounds might not be out of the question. Call it blackmail. Call it a mere business proposition. It's all the same. But would it be worth the confrontation, exposure to possible prosecution?

He made his decision. He'd do it, but not be too greedy. He tossed off his second drink. He took out three sheets of paper and pen and ink from the drawer and began writing notes, each similar but with variations for the different individuals to receive them, the common denominator being that he was offering a commodity valuable to each of them at the same price. The amount, he finally decided, would be three thousand pounds.

He sealed the letters and put them into envelopes. Just time enough to take them down and slip them under the doors; then he must prepare for the next show. But before going down to nine, he first had to find a better hiding place. He took the bundle from the drawer and looked about the room at the boxes and storage cabinets along the wall.

When Ernest Hemingway and Mary Miles Minter strolled from the showroom, he wondered how he could stretch out the evening with her. He had more than one thing he wanted to talk with her about. As the elevator reached the ground floor, he turned to her. "I was surprised your mother allowed us this much time," he teased, "considering your age. Is it past your bedtime?"

She scowled. "Ernest! I'm not a child. I'm—eighteen! She said to be back by eleven. That gives us another hour."

"Eighteen. Hmmm." He smiled. "All right, then. A stroll down the Champs-Elysees?"

"With your legs—and a cane?"

He smiled. "I can hobble. Just don't run away from me."

She took his left arm with her two hands. "I'll hang on."

He was silent as they slowly crossed the lobby to the street and went outside. "Cloudy now. It might rain."

Mary gathered her coat about her more snugly.

Hemingway said, "Your mother seemed receptive to me."

"That's my mother for you. She doesn't see you as a threat to what she wants for me. I'm not even sure what that is. But you'll be coming back here, to Paris. I'll be safely stuck in Hollywood again. We'll be five or six thousand miles apart."

"I sensed that she checks out anyone you meet very carefully."

Mary frowned at him as they walked slowly down the promenade toward the distant Arc de Triomphe. "She has some reason, I suppose. I had what you writers call a *liaison*, in Hollywood, with an older man." She laughed. "Much older."

"And what do you want to tell me about him?"

She tried to keep her voice light as she said, "He's a movie director. He remade me to his liking; then he fell in love with me, and I with him—at least I thought I did. But he has someone else now." She frowned, then looked up at him with a quick smile. "And I have you."

Hemingway could feel the hurt in her voice, despite her words and expression. "Will you see him when you return?"

She nodded. "I must. He'll direct some of my movies."

"At least you're at ease enough to talk about it."

"Yes, but let's not. I'd rather talk about you. And me."

Hemingway thought for a moment. "Well, there are one or two little things."

Mary looked at him. "You want me to do something for you. I can tell."

"You were at that party held by Martin Prince. I wonder if you could help me get an interview with him. I want to do important interviews. Even political leaders, like Clemenceau, someday. It could help my career."

Mary nodded. "I'll ask Mother. She's closer to him. But I'm sure it can be done."

"Good. And the other thing. The Professor—the paranormal Investigator? You know him."

"I don't know him that well."

"But he knows you're an actress, someone important."

"What do you want, Ernest?"

"I want to get more information about this case for that article I mentioned. If you could put in a word . . ."

"All right. Whenever I see him." She paused. "Now, you do something for me."

"Anything."

"Tell me about how you grew up. Your childhood. I want to know everything. Starting with what you ate for breakfast."

Martin Prince sat in a large easy chair, one hand holding a whiskey glass. Patricia August sat oppposite on the plush sofa. Mixed feelings plagued him. He wondered how much he could confide in her now, despite their usual closeness. Fitch had muddied the water. Was he conspiring with her against him?

He knew the trip to Paris would be seen as a catastrophe by his board of directors. Although he held great sway as Editorial Director, he could be replaced with new ownership. The sword Fitch held, if he bought that stock, would always be over his head. What else could go wrong? Murder. Investigations. Books he was counting on to be worthwhile by Edda Van Eych and Camilo were not panning out. His English publisher, Tyler, in obvious need of replacment with someone vigorous, but Tyler not liking it. The millionaire Fitch nibbling at his back. Was the man— so confident—talking to his board? And what about Trisha?

Prince shook his head to get rid of the cobwebs. "Fill this up again, Trisha. And don't be stingy."

She took his glass to the bar in the corner of the room and refilled it, also topping off her own glass of champagne. She returned and handed his glass to him. "Problems, Martin? You're very subdued tonight, not your usual self."

He glared at her. "You'd like to have my job, wouldn't you? Well, by God, you may get a chance at it!" He waved a hand. "No, don't deny it. That's the way it works. Climb up the ladder, then it gets shaky, and you fall off. You look down. Someone is climbing up behind you. Someone else is shaking the ladder."

"Martin, if you're doubting my loyalty—"

"No, no. It's not you. It's just—nothing's going right."

"The murder."

"That. Everything. Things I can't tell you. The trip was too soon. I should have waited a year to come here. Europe will be ready then. There's still too much hostility in the air over here."

"I know what it is—your books aren't going well, are they?"

He nodded, and took a large swallow of his whiskey. "The board is expecting big things, now that the war's over."

"It will come. A lot of it will come from Paris. Writers will be here, turning out masterpieces. It takes time."

"I hope so. The young woman—Sylvia Beach—she thinks so."

"And I do too, Martin."

"I know I was harsh with them—the Dutch woman, and the Spaniard."

"You're honest."

He shook his head. "I've been in this business long enough to know they'd rather have dishonesty with a check, instead of an honest appraisal of their work and no check. Money and a kind word is the perfect combination. But they'll give up the kind word for the money."

"And if they can have neither?"

"I don't know. Maybe they get violent. Writers can, you know. Maybe they kill people. Who knows why Thorndyke was murdered?"

"Yes, Martin. Who knows? And who will find out why?"

Prince finished his glass and leaned back. "Go on now. Sorry I was a little rough. I'll just sit here for a while. Think about things. Maybe I'll get a brain wave, a good idea."

Trisha picked up the glasses and put them on the bar. She walked about, switching off a lamp here and another there, leaving only one lit. Then she stepped quietly into the hall.

After she left, Prince heard a slight noise at the hall door. He stepped over to the door, picked up the envelope from the floor, ripped it open, and read it quickly. By the time he peered out into the hallway it was deserted.

Penny Darnell slipped her shoes off and lay on the bed in their room. "Come here, John, lie beside me."

He looked at his watch. Ten-thirty. He stepped

over and sat on the side of the bed. "I have to patrol the corridor in about an hour."

"Your ghost, of course."

"Not mine, but I hope whoever it is shows up again tonight."

"Whoever? Then you think—"

"Someone is pretending to be a ghost. That's certain enough. The question is why."

"And who, right?"

He scowled. "If I can grab him, I'll find out who, soon enough."

"John, could the ghost be someone in Prince's party, one of his entourage of writers, publishers? They seem unlikely."

"Let's consider that. I think we can eliminate the women—Edda Van Eych, Mrs. Fitch, Patricia August, the actress and her mother. The ghost was definitely a man."

"And that leaves?"

He ticked them off. "Philip Thorndyke, first."

"The son? But why?"

"I don't know why anyone would do it yet. But he looks a lot like his father. Then there's Martin Prince himself, and Fitch, Camilo, Tyler, and Ward."

"Ward? A bit hefty, isn't he?"

"Yes, but one of them could pass for Thorndyke, late at night in the shadows of the hall, wearing similar clothing. I realized it during the show tonight, how important the clothing is. It's the clothing that does it, I'm convinced of that. Thorndyke's clothing."

"Sort of a—well, a suggestion, of his appearance."

"Exactly."

She pulled him down beside her. "Your ghost only walks at midnight, John. We have an hour to ourselves. And we *are* in Paris." She put her arms around him and pressed her lips on his.

The killer sat in the room in the dark, staring out of the windows at the panorama of Paris lights and the Eiffel Tower in the distance. The silence was tangible. Thoughts of the killing raged through the murderer's mind. Was it the only way? The letter and envelope told the story. Others had certainly received the note. It had to be done without delay.

If things could be done over, could there have been any other alternative? The answer always was no, and the time to act now, before it was too late.

The figure picked up an object from the table and looked at it in the ambient light from the street below, angling through the windows into the dark room. A simple device, a thong of strong leather, an elongated knob tied at each end. The killer held one end in each hand and stretched it taut. The question that came—*Shall I use this again?*—brought a twisted smile. But the bitter, answering thought—*You know damn well you must!*—erased every vestige of the smile.

The killer rose, walked to the door, and peered out into the deserted hotel corridor. It was time.

Darnell stood in the same alcove he had used for concealment the night before. Already midnight, and nothing had appeared. The occupants of the other rooms on the ninth floor had retired for the night, perhaps regarding it as the better part of valor to give the uninvited guest full sway on the floor. He had known all along the intruder was a fraud, as all supposed ghosts were. But now he connected the evil of the one action, the deception, with the reality of the other, the killing. Solve one, catch the Thorndyke look-alike wearing the dead man's clothes, and learn much. How had he obtained the clothes? Why is he doing this? Is he really the killer after all?

Darnell was beginning to feel that whoever was masquerading as the ghost of Eric Thorndyke had decided the investigations made his impersonation too perilous now. He doubted that anyone would show up that night, or any other night. But at his last moment of doubt, a swirl of gray smoke appeared opposite suite 999 and the vision suddenly was there—the ghostly looking man, just as the soldier had described him the night before, Darnell seeing him with his own eyes for the first time. Through the smoke he caught flashes of the red tie and cummerbund.

The smoke billowed as Darnell ran toward the spot, but when he reached it he found nothing there. The door to the stairwell moved slightly, apparently swinging back into place, as it had the night before. He ran to it, pushed it open, and charged down the stairs, but in a moment saw that no one had preceded him.

Darnell listened. The stairway below was silent. He returned to the ninth-floor landing and came to the realization at that instant. The stairway continued up one floor to the penthouse tenth-floor level. The ghost's escape route was up, not down. And it was too late to apprehend him now.

He returned to their room and found Penny asleep. In minutes he was lying beside her, but not sleeping, staring at the ceiling, thinking the experience

through. He had missed him, yes, and probably for
the first and last time. The fox would go to ground
now. But now he knew what he must do the next
day.

Chapter Ten

Saturday morning, December 28

Darnell left Penny in their room to dress and prepare to meet her friend Sylvia for breakfast and an outing in Paris. He took the elevator down to the mezzanine and entered Jacques Bardon's office five minutes before the appointed time of nine a.m. In addition to meeting Bardon's Chairman—who had engaged him on this case—and Inspector Manot's superior officer, he planned to propose a new meeting to advance the case. It would be a busy day.

Bardon's secretary greeted him with a bright, "Good morning, Professor. The others have just arrived. Go right in."

After rapping twice on the door, he entered Bardon's private office. The four men were standing, still being introduced.

"Come in, Professor Darnell," Bardon said, and included him in the introduction process. Darnell was not surprised to see that Chairman Beauvais was a well-dressed, corpulent man and that Chief Inspector Guerin was an older, white-haired version of Inspector Manot.

Chairman Beauvais of Le Grand Hotel fixed his

gaze on Darnell. "The case, *mon ami*, it goes well? Tell me all."

Darnell shook hands with him. "Thank you for the case, Chairman. It is very interesting. If you don't mind, I'll address my remarks to both you and the Chief Inspector, and to the others, to save time."

The Chairman nodded. "We are ready."

Guerin said, "Inspector Manot has told me, briefly, of the interviews. I am anxious to hear more."

"There are two mysteries, of course," Darnell said, "the murder and the ghost." He included each of them in his gaze, watching their reactions. "Both mysteries are part of the same overall puzzle. Let's take the murder of Eric Thorndyke first. The problem is in one sense complicated by the considerable number of potential suspects. A dozen of them. And yet, by the other token, the precise number of guests in Martin Prince's entourage also tends to limit the likely suspects to those specific people, although, theoretically, someone else in the hotel could have committed the murder."

Chief Inspector Guerin said, "We did not want to interrogate every guest in the hotel."

"Exactly. Now, as to the so-called ghost, it's clear that some man is passing himself off as Thorndyke's ghost for reasons we don't yet understand. He dresses precisely as Thorndyke did the night of the fatal party. In fact, I believe he is wearing the clothes Thorndyke wore the night of the murder. He has obtained the clothes, and therefore puts on the good impression of being him. Chances are his facial appearance is really not that close to Thorndyke's. The first night we arrived here, there was a sighting of him by a young soldier. I missed that one, but last night I saw him myself."

The four men exhanged glances. Manot said, "You pursued him?"

"Yes, but he vanished. After running down the stairs in pursuit, I realized he had fled *upstairs*, going to the tenth floor, the penthouse."

"But there are no residence rooms up there," Bardon said, "other than the owner's suite." He looked at Chairman Beauvais. "And one other—the performer's room, next to the showroom."

"I let no one use my room," the Chairman said. "And I was not here last night. It is fully secured."

"Back to the murder for a moment, gentlemen. It was committed by a most unusual method—the garrote. Obviously, that tended to train suspicion on the Spaniard, Camilo, since the garrote is of Spanish origin."

The Chief Inspector said, "But . . . ?"

Darnell said, "Precisely. It would be rather naive of him to use a weapon so closely associated with his own country, instead of a nonspecific method such as a knife. The garrote was used possibly to cast suspicion on Camilo. To divert suspicion from the killer."

Chairman Beauvais glanced around the room at the others. "Is that definite?"

"No, because by reverse logic, the Spaniard would know the use of it would tend to show his innocence, because it would be so obvious in pointing to his guilt."

The Inspector nodded. "Clever, if the Spaniard is, in fact, so clever. If not, it's simply a mistake. But I don't see where your reasoning is taking us. Chief Inspector?"

"Let him continue. We cover, how they say, all the bases?"

Darnell went on. "We learn. We learn of peculiarities in relationships among the parties in this group, things to think about. Putting together the disjointed comments of Prince's invited guests from our interviews, an overall picture emerges. Eric Thorndyke had some special project he was offering, but Prince was not interested. The Dutch woman, Edda Van Eych, was presenting a book to Prince that he declined. The Spaniard was working on a book Prince felt was unrealistic. Prince's contractual publisher contact in England was perhaps about to be terminated and then—"

Inspector Manot interrupted. "What are you saying?"

"Looking at the motives discovered so far, it appears the bad feelings here were largely directed, not at Thorndyke, but at Martin Prince himself."

The Inspector snorted. "Are you suggesting the wrong man was murdered? Is it possible?"

"We can't ignore the possibility," Darnell said. "Thorndyke was killed in Prince's spare bedroom, the only one leading from the hall. If he was murdered by a hired killer—"

The Chief Inspector said, "There could have been confusion."

"And if he was killed by one of the guests—well, it seems like most of them had a motive to kill Prince."

Chairman Beauvais spoke up. "So you are again back to the beginning, *n'est-ce pas?*"

"Not quite. We look at everything. I've met all the players now. But I want to talk with Philip Thorndyke again, in more depth. We must find the motive for Thorndyke's murder. I think Philip will know it, whether he realizes it or not. I want to ask him about his father's clothing. We need to dispose of the question of whether Thorndyke could have been murdered by mistake. I don't have an opinion on it—but we have to know. And I want to meet and interview one other person today who may be able to help my thought process. I want to meet Adrian, the magician who performs in your showroom, Chairman."

"The showroom," Manot said. "On the tenth floor."

"Yes," Darnell answered. "With the performer's room next to it. Where Adrian could have run to last night when I lost him."

Beauvais raised his eyebrows. "Adrian is the ghost?"

"I believe it's likely, now, after last night."

Beauvais nodded at Bardon. "Consider it done. Jacques will take you to Adrian. And if he's guilty of this—"

Manot said, "If he's guilty he'll land in jail."

"And never work here again," Bardon said.

Beauvais stood. "There are but three days left before the eve of the New Year. We must have this all settled by then."

Darnell nodded. "Today we may see a turning point."

Penny Darnell and Sylvia Beach walked across the lobby of Le Grand. "You'll be interested in meeting these two," Sylvia said. "I knew the girl from the Prince party, and she introduced me to her new friend down here last night after dinner. A soldier."

"They're having breakfast with us?"

"And a short stroll through the Tuileries Gardens, if they want to join us. He uses a cane. War injuries."

"Sorry to hear that."

Penny looked ahead and saw the tall young man

leaning on a cane at the exit leading out to the Champs-Elysees. A young blond woman rested one hand in the crook of his free arm.

Sylvia made the introductions. "Penny, meet Ernest Hemingway and Mary Miles Minter. This is Penny Darnell, Professor Darnell's wife." They shook hands before stepping out onto the sidewalk.

Hemingway said, "I'm glad to meet you, Mrs. Darnell. I've been wanting to talk with your husband. I saw him the first night I checked in, you know."

"Yes, the ghost. He told me."

"I'm writing an article about all this. I'm a reporter—that is, I was one and will be one again when I go home."

"You want to talk with him?"

"Maybe for ten, fifteen minutes. I know he's busy."

"I'll talk with him as soon as I see him."

Hemingway thanked her, and shook her hand again.

Sylvia said, "The clouds warn of rain, but let's brave it."

Sylvia Beach led them over a bridge across the Seine to a small restaurant on the Left Bank. "Good breakfasts here," she said, as they took seats at a window table. When the waiter served coffee, she nodded at Mary and Hemingway. "They'll have Kir."

Mary looked at Sylvia. "Kir? What's that?"

"A splash of *cassis*—a berry juice—and the glass filled with dry white wine. You and Ernest should try it."

"With breakfast?"

Hemingway smiled. "Older children in France are given wine by their parents. It's a custom. And it's a late breakfast."

Mary glowered at Hemingway at the word "children." When the waiter poured kir for Hemingway and her, she tasted it. "Mmmm."

"It's good," Hemingway said. He spoke again of his experience in the hallway the night he encountered Darnell. "Certainly looked like a ghost to me."

Penny nodded. "John doesn't argue with what people see."

Mary Minter asked, "How does the Professor investigate? All I know is what I see on the movie sets and on the screen. A hawk-nosed man with a magnifying glass."

Penny laughed. "He'd like that part about the hawk nose. Yet he has been known to use a magnifying glass sometimes. I tease him about looking like Sherlock Holmes when he does."

Hemingway followed her words closely. "And his methods?"

"Mostly, I think, he tries to understand the psychology and philosophy of the suspects—of all the people involved in the case."

"Like a writer would do? Understanding the characters?"

"I suppose, yes. But what he's really doing is applying the same principles of the studies he teaches. That's why he calls himself a "psychichologist," because the psychology is often applied to the apparent psychic phenomena that bring him into a case. In his approach, it's as much a question of *why*, as well as *who*, that reveals the truth. Once into a case—well, he often deals with the crime as well as the reported supernatural incidents, because the crime is usually right there, under the surface, and intertwined with the supposed psychic phenomenon."

"Like in Mr. Thorndyke's killing," Mary said, shivering.

"Everything in the case is related. John sorts it out."

In an effort to change the direction of the conversation, Sylvia Beach asked Hemingway, "What kind of writing do you do, Ernest? Mary said you were a writer."

The young soldier stared into his wineglass. "Before the war—that seems years ago, already—I worked as a reporter for the *Kansas City Star*. That's where I really learned to write."

"What do you mean by that?"

"How to write with concrete, specific images and concise language. I add my own style, a certain emphasis and repetition in my wording that I hope will mesmerize. And you need drama. You have to pay the bills even while trying for artistic purity."

"So . . . you want to be a reporter?"

He shook his head. "Only as an opening, a beginning to something else. This story about the hotel, the ghost, the murder—that would make good copy. I could get a start with it. But later, well, I want to walk these streets with good legs, and write about Paris. There's a beautiful, wistful, elegant sadness about this city. I want to write about the love that's here. And I want to write about the war, too, and how it destroyed the moral standards of my generation, of those who managed to stay alive—the lost generation."

Sylvia nodded. *"Une generation purdu."*

Mary Miles Minter put a hand on Hemingway's. "Lost, maybe. But I found him. And he found me."

Penny and Sylvia exchanged a smile.

Sylvia said, "*Amourette*," smiled, and whispered in Penny's ear. "Puppy love."

"Paris is having its effect, war or not," Penny said.

Hemingway smiled. "It's more free here in Paris. In America—well, in my family at least—there's a strictness that holds you back. Here I can write."

Sylvia said, "Paris does free you. It's the air, I think, and the moonlight glistening on the Seine, the profile of La Tour Eiffel against the night sky. And now the war is over, romantics of the world will come here, and the intellectuals will meet in salons, and they'll all write about life."

"And you?" Penny asked. "What will you do, Sylvia?"

Sylvia's eyes sparkled. "I'll sell the books they write from my own little bookstore."

Chapter Eleven

Late Saturday morning, December 28

Bardon led the way to Adrian's tenth-floor room. When the magician answered the door, minus the moustache and Van Dyke beard and looking as if he had just left his bed, Bardon said, "May we enter? These gentlemen have a few questions for you."

Adrian looked from Manot to Darnell. "And they are . . . ?"

"Inspector Manot and Professor John Darnell. They are investigating the death that occurred early last week."

He nodded. "Come in. But I don't know what I can say on that."

Bardon said, "I leave you then to your questions." He left the room, and Adrian motioned toward chairs.

"You begin, Professor," Manot said.

When they were seated, Darnell said, "You arrived at the hotel for your tour here, exactly when?"

"December fifteenth. My performances began the next night."

"You've heard about the murder, of course."

"I'm sure everyone in the hotel knows of it."

"And the ghost, you're aware of that, ah, little phenomenon?"

He looked down. "Ye-es."

"The ghost bears a remarkable resemblance to yourself—absent your stage facial hair." Darnell watched his expression.

Manot glanced at Darnell with raised eyebrows.

Adrian touched his upper lip and chin. "I remove the beard and moustache after my performances. But you say, resemblance? I'm a rather average man."

"As is our ghost, sir."

"But what are you suggesting?"

"Perhaps you're amusing yourself by passing yourself off as a ghost. Expanding your magic out into the hallways."

Adrian sputtered. "Preposterous! Yes, I'm a performer, but I'm not a fool."

Manot said, "The hotel guests have been upset. More than one checked out as a result. It's time to tell us the truth."

"I know nothing of it."

Manot glared at Adrian. "There could be a crime here."

Adrian jumped to his feet, but immmediately sat down again. "You're upsetting me." He looked deliberately at Darnell. "Find your damned ghost yourself! That's what you do, isn't it?"

"You claim you know nothing about it," Darnell said.

"That is the truth." Adrian brushed his hair back with both hands, and seemed to gather strength. "And now, if you'll excuse me, I have some rehearsing to do. I must plan for the last performance in a few days and my big, final act."

Manot said, "If what you say is a lie, and if all this is your doing, I'll have your final act for you. You disappear!"

Adrian set his jaw. "I am a performer. Not a criminal."

The men left Adrian's room and stood in the hall discussing the magician's protestations. "He's lying," Darnell said. "We know now he was the ghost. But why?"

"I did not expect him to confess."

"The point is, he may be lying about more than one thing."

"So, he could even be the killer, if he has a motive."

"Our interview will do one thing, I can assure you, Inspector. There will be no more ghosts at Le Grand Hotel. This magician's skillful impersonations, for whatever reason they existed, are now ended. And my job, too, will be over."

"We still have a murder to solve."

"We?"

Manot smiled, for the first time with what Darnell thought to be genuine humor. "You know too much, and you have too many ideas to get away that easily. I'm sure Chairman Beauvais would agree. The cloud of murder still hangs over his hotel."

"If you're sure—"

"I am certain. Now let us see Philip Thorndyke one more time, as you suggested."

Stepping from the elevator, Manot said to Darnell, "How did you guess Adrian was the ghost? Did you recognize him from the one time you saw him?"

"No. But after I saw the so-called ghost and he escaped to the tenth floor, it was a hunch. A magician and an impersonator both depend upon illusion. The ghostly appearance was achieved largely by costume—the clothing. Adrian uses costumes for effect. That's my thought now—to find out about the ghost's clothes."

When they reached Philip Thorndyke's suite, they found him there, as if in a cocoon, as Darnell expected. Remains of a tray of food, largely untouched, sat on a table.

"I'm getting tired of room service," the young man said. "Tonight I'm going to dine at Armand's."

"You resume life," Darnell said.

"Yes. I have to think of other things."

"Then my questions and requests won't bother you unduly?"

He sat back and looked at Darnell. "What are they?"

"You've not indicated what you thought might be a motive for your father's death. Could he have been killed by mistake, by a misunderstanding?"

"I don't know . . . What do you mean?"

"I think we established it was most likely that someone entered from the corridor. If the killer thought the man in that room was someone else, like Martin Prince . . ."

"And murdered him under a misbelief?"

"It was Prince's suite. The killer may have thought Prince was the man in that chair—his party, his suite, his bedroom."

"But that would mean the killer was not someone in Prince's party. Everyone in this group knew my father was in there."

"A hired killer might not know, or might have been confused under the circumstances. It is merely a possible explanation."

"You know my offer of payment still stands," Philip Thorndyke said to Darnell. "I'll firm it up. Find my father's killer, Professor, and I'll pay you an additional five thousand dollars."

Darnell frowned. "Before we go too far, there are some other small matters."

"Yes?"

"You suggested during our first meeting that when you entered Prince's bedroom, they heard you call out."

"Did I say that?"

"Others say the door was closed."

Philip Thorndyke swallowed and stared at Darnell. "I came out, I cried out. I don't know the sequence."

"Could the door have been closed?"

"Maybe. I knew he was seriously drunk. Didn't want others to see him that way. Maybe I closed it." He stared at Darnell. "You're saying you suspect me! Is that it? That I went in there and killed my own father?"

Darnell shook his head. "We just need the facts on these small matters straight, to get at the truth."

Philip Thorndyke scowled. "Any other . . . *small matters*?"

"One. The ghost."

"That's your specialty."

"I think you might know something about it. The clothing the ghost has been wearing is exactly like your father's clothes. In fact, I think it is his clothes."

Philip Thorndyke looked at them. "So now you think I'm acting as the ghost? The answer is, I can't tell you anything."

Manot said, "If you don't tell us now, you might be held accountable for withholding evidence in a murder case. You don't want a criminal offense, do you?"

Thorndyke cringed. He looked around, as if wanting a drink. Sighing, he said at last, "All right. I'll tell you this much. It had nothing to do with the murder, except my crazy idea—if I had a ghost show up, the murderer might get nervous and do something to give himself away. I know it's far-fetched, but it's all I could think of to do."

"You supplied the clothing," Darnell said.

"Yes."

"To whom?"

"That's all you're getting. It's not important who."

Darnell nodded. "We think we know. We'll come back to that. One other thing, right now."

"What?"

"You have your father's effects. The things found on his, ah, body."

"All of his things are in his bedroom. The *Sûreté* has gone through them."

"Then you won't mind if I do the same?"

The young man raised both hands. "Look through them." He took a deep breath. "I—I'm sorry if I've been a bit sharp."

"It's understandable." Darnell nodded at the closed bedroom door. "Then we may inspect the room?"

Philip Thorndyke responded by walking to the bedroom door and throwing it open. "Everything's here. It's all yours."

"He was working on a special project—a book? Something like that?"

"Ye-es?"

"Is it here?"

Thorndyke mumbled, "Whatever it is, it's gone."

"And what is it, precisely?"

"A script of some kind for a motion picture. I never saw it, but I wish I had it right now." He paused. "Anything else?"

"No. We'll look through his things, then."

"All right. And while you're looking, I'm leaving. I need some fresh air. I'm going to take a long walk on the Champs-Elysees. I've seen enough of this hotel for a lifetime."

As the hall door banged behind Philip Thorndyke, Darnell scowled. "I agree with him. I just realized I haven't set foot outside of this hotel since we checked in. I'm wanting some of that fresh air he spoke of. Getting stale here. I'm used to prowling the streets of London sometimes, even in the fog, to clear my head."

Manot said, "Go out, then. Refresh your thoughts."

"Yes . . . but right now, we have work to do." Darnell glanced about the bedroom, removed his coat, and stepped over to a dresser. "I'll start here, if you'll take the closet."

"I'll do it again, but my men have inspected this room."

"They no doubt looked for the extraordinary, for a garrote, I expect, that sort of thing. We won't find that. I'm interested in the obvious—concealed by its ordinariness."

The two men began their methodical search. Darnell opened each drawer and looked through the contents meticulously. Manot turned out the pockets of every coat and pair of trousers in the closet, and left each pocket turned out as evidence of his search, and to be sure every garment had been examined.

They proceeded on through the nightstand, looking into two suitcases that sat in the corner of the room, inspecting the implements and supplies in the bathroom. They moved any items of interest into a group on a table in the center of the room. Finished, Darnell and Manot stared down at the small accumulation.

"Not much," Manot said. "The clothes offered surprisingly little."

Darnell inspected the collection. A journal with jottings an author might make as notes to himself. Business cards from some of the others in the entourage—the publisher Tyler, millionaire Fitch, and Prince. English and French coins and currency. A pen and a bottle of ink. A pair of reading glasses. Keys on a ring. Two loose keys.

Manot said, "I'm sure we saw all this and returned it to the son."

"There are some things missing, of course."

"Missing?"

"The clothes—the red bow tie, the red cummerbund. We know about them."

"Yes."

Darnell picked up the journal. "Did you read this?"

Manot nodded. "Nothing incriminating."

"May I take it? I'd like to read it."

"Of course. It is still evidence in a sense, available to me. But I'll advise Philip you have it."

Darnell inspected the ring of keys, one at a time. "A home in England . . . an office . . . a motorcar." He picked up the loose keys and looked at Manot. "And these?"

"The larger, ornate key is for the main door to the suite. That small key opens the corridor entrance."

Darnell nodded. "So every suite has one room, like

this bedroom, that is opened from the outer corridor by key."

"Like Prince's room. Where Thorndyke was killed."

"And the question being, did someone have a key to that door?"

When the elevator reached the ninth floor, Adrian glanced both ways up and down the corridor, making sure no one was in the hallway, before stepping out of the car. He didn't want to be observed going to Philip Thorndyke's room. Seeing the way was clear, he quickly headed down the corridor. Halfway there, he saw Thorndyke's door open and the young man enter the corridor and walk in his direction. He stopped and waited for him.

As Thorndyke approached, he slowed and, reaching Adrian, asked, "What do you want?"

"We have to talk."

Philip Thorndyke grimaced. "All right, but not here. If you insist on doing this, you can meet me outside."

"Where?"

"I was on my way out for a walk. Take the elevator down, go out to the boulevard and turn right, go down one block to your right, to the corner. I'll follow in the next elevator car."

Adrian nodded, pressed the button to call an elevator and waited for it. When it arrived he entered it and the door closed.

Five minutes later, Thorndyke walked up to Adrian, who stood on a corner a block away, leaning against a building, reading a magazine from a stand. Adrian put the magazine back and fell into step with Thorndyke who strode by him without pausing.

"Now," Thorndyke said, sidelong, "what's on your mind?"

"This thing is getting out of hand. The Inspector and that meddling Professor have been quizzing me, and I don't like it."

"They sniff about. It's their nature."

"The Professor's onto me."

"So, stop, then. It isn't working anyway."

"Of course, I'll *stop*! I'm not a goddamn fool. It's over, as of this moment. Everyone will be out there tonight, looking for your—your stupid ghost! For me!"

Thorndyke suddenly halted in his stride. Adrian stumbled as he brought himself up short, and turned back to him. They stood next to a building out of the pedestrian traffic flow.

Thorndyke said to him, "You want something. Spill it."

Adrian looked about the wide walkway at passersby moving in both directions. "Of course I do. A larger fee. Call it a termination bonus. You've been paying me a pittance, and now the police are investigating me. You can just double it now."

Philip Thorndyke's eyes widened. "Double . . . ?" He scowled, looked away from Adrian, looked up and down the street. "You're getting greedy."

Adrian's lips turned up slyly at the corners, as he observed Thorndyke's reaction. "The Inspector would forgive my little play-acting to learn the entire truth about this affair." When Thorndyke said nothing, he decided to play his other card. "And another thing," he said, pausing, waiting for the raised eyebrows, enjoying the moment. He took a sheet of paper from his pocket and held it down at his side.

"What have you got there?"

"Did you receive my note last night?"

"Yes."

"I just happen to have what it seems everybody in this hotel is looking for. I've offered it for a price, but I'm thinking, maybe, the highest bidder gets it."

"And proof that you have it?"

Adrian held the single sheet of paper up in front of Philip Thorndyke's face, but not close enough for the other to grasp it.

"My God! It looks like a script! Is that really it?"

"The genuine article."

"You stole it!"

"Never mind that. Let's talk about the money. First, let's finish up with my impersonation job. My fee? Doubled?"

Thorndyke pulled out a flat wallet from his jacket pocket and removed some hundred-pound notes. "Here's three hundred pounds more. Now we're done. Six hundred pounds is a lot of money for what you did."

"Good. A man of honor. Now, on the other matter. The script."

"It belongs to me. It's my father's. That's theft."

"Maybe he gave it to me, Philip. Maybe I bought it. And, as to ownership, there's no name on the cover now. I took care of that. Think of it as if I've just had it in safekeeping for you. But whatever I charge, you can sell it for more. There's a market for this script, I'm sure. I've read it."

Thorndyke was silent for a moment. He sighed. "How much are you asking?"

"You read the note. Three thousand pounds. I keep my word." He smiled. "Unless I get a better offer."

Thorndyke's brows furrowed. "The Inspector and the Professor are in my rooms right now. They like to poke about. I can't go back there, can't get that much money on the weekend." He considered. "I'll go to the bank Monday morning. Come to my room after your show Monday night—after eleven."

Adrian smiled. "That's it, then. I can wait."

"And if someone else offers more?"

"I'll let you know. Wouldn't want you to miss the bidding."

"All right. Now go back to the hotel, or go to hell! I want to walk. Alone." Thorndyke strode off, not looking back.

Adrian watched him walk away for a moment, then headed back in the direction of Le Grand. As he walked, he folded up the sheet, pocketed it once more, and smiled.

Chapter Twelve

Mary Miles Minter held on to Ernest Hemingway's free arm as they strolled down the Champs-Elysees at a hobbling pace. He wanted to see the Arc de Triomphe close up, he said, and after separating from Penny Darnell and Sylvia Beach, they walked there.

They both put their hands on its facing. "We touched it," Mary said. They soon headed back, glancing in shop windows, talking, working their way toward the hotel. Hemingway was eager to get started on what he considered a little investigation of his own, but he was hungry again. They took a table at a sidewalk café where he ordered a sandwich and Mary took coffee and a croissant.

She watched him take large bites, enjoying his food. "Fishing, hunting, then—that's what you liked, growing up?"

"Good roast beef," he said, between mouthfuls.

"Tell me about yourself."

"I liked the outdoors. My sister was a tomboy, and we were pals. I shot a blue heron once. She was amazed. I liked football, sports. And boxing—I was pretty good. Canoeing. I liked to rough it. Camped quite a bit." He took a huge bite of his sandwich and said, "Talk about yourself, while I eat."

"Oh—I like colorful things, blues, reds, and soft things, laces, and like that. I'd be a very domestic girl, if I had the time, if I wasn't doing moving pictures. I'd read . . ."

"What?"

"I like Edgar Allan Poe, the Rubaiyat, Shelley, Keats, Byron. But I'm domestic—I like to cook, wash dishes, and darn socks."

He laughed. "Mary Miles Minter darning socks. That would make the headlines!"

"But it's true. I'm sort of a recluse now. They call me the hermit girl of the screen. I don't mingle. But I could be a good wife." She looked at him. "To the right gentleman."

He concentrated on his food. "When did you begin acting?"

"I was on the stage for a while, at age five. I remember my first stage role—Toinette. Then I went into movies." Mary laughed. "When I went to the studios with my mother and saw pictures, I thought the actors and actresses stood behind the screen and they played a light on them for the images. Soon I was a fairy in one."

"Order some more coffee, fairy." He smiled.

When the waiter refilled their cups, she said, "Someone poisoned my poodle, Woof-Woof, last year."

"That's terrible. I follow bullfights. It's one thing to kill a bull . . . but a poodle?"

"I don't see the difference."

"It's the bull's destiny. He knows what he must do."

They were silent for a moment or two. "Have you seen any of my motion pictures?"

"Just one, *Dimples*. I liked it."

He paid the bill and they headed toward the Le Grand Hotel, but he glanced at his watch, other things clearly on his mind now. "My appointment with Mr. Prince is in a half hour, thanks to your mother. And I'm sure I'll be seeing the Professor soon. I want to get going on this story. It could be important."

Mary nodded absently, serious now. "If I could only be that optimistic. But a week from now we'll be back in our own lives, and you won't be thinking of me, and I—"

"You'll be making more pictures that move people."

Hemingway leaned down and kissed her lightly. But as he did, he knew it might be the only time he would, that the prologue of their relationship was already an epilogue, that their romance would be over before it began.

At the hotel, Mary left Hemingway at the front entrance. He headed straight to the elevators, stepping off on the ninth floor for his appointment with Martin Prince. He hobbled across the corridor to the door of Martin Prince's suite with some trepidation. At only nineteen years, about to speak to a world-renowned editor, he felt qualms. Such a man would probably decline an interview, he thought, even though Mary Minter's mother had made this appointment. Prince would give him a few minutes as a courtesy and then brush him off.

Hemingway sighed. But he knew he'd always regret it if he didn't at least try. He took a deep breath and prepared to knock on the door, but withdrew his hand, seeing the door slightly ajar. He peered through the narrow opening, and was startled when he saw a man's head leaning over the back of a chair, in pain, or injured or . . .

He could not determine what, but was concerned now, and knocked loudly on the door. It swung in at the pressure, and now he could see the scene more clearly. It had to be Martin Prince sprawled in an easy chair, his head back, with an angry red gash all around his neck. Although he was compelled to see the man closer, Hemingway had no real doubt now. This was a dead body.

With his limp and cane as impediments, he hobbled over to the body as quickly as he could. He put two fingers on Martin Prince's neck and nodded. "Dead," he said aloud, the word sounding hollow in the empty room. He looked around. No one else there. But as he straightened up, he was shocked by a stifled scream from behind him at the doorway. He jerked his head around to see a woman standing there with a hand covering her mouth.

"You killed him!" she shrieked. She took a step backward, in obvious fear.

"No, no," Hemingway protested. "I just walked in, believe me. I've never met him. I found him just like this, just now." He moved toward her in his faltering gait.

"Stop! Right there." She looked at him as he halted.

"I'm innocent, believe me."

"Then who are you? Explain yourself."

"I was going to interview him. I'm a, well, a journalist."

The woman looked Hemingway up and down, evidently taking in the fact that he was a soldier. "He's—he's really dead, then?"

Hemingway nodded. "I'm afraid so."

"We have to call the Manager and the police."

She stumbled to a chair opposite Prince's body and stared at Hemingway. "Call the desk. Please."

Hemingway stepped over to the telephone and spoke into it. "They'll be up in a minute." Aware the hall door still stood open, he closed it and stood against it. "My name is Ernest Hemingway. Who are you?"

Even as he spoke, Hemingway was thinking of the magnitude of the event and what it might mean to him as a reporter. He considered the story he wanted to write, discovering a body, maybe interviewing the people.

She looked up at him, clearly still stunned. "I'm his associate, Patricia August." She turned again and stared at Martin Prince. "He was murdered. Look at that deep wound in his neck. God! Just like Thorndyke." Tears filled her eyes. "Poor Martin. I can't believe it."

Hemingway moved toward her. At first she shrank back, until she saw he was offering her a white handkerchief, and took it from him. He resumed his journalist role, seeing this as his chance. "Had you seen him this morning?"

She dabbed at her eyes. "No. He was a notoriously late sleeper. Stayed up to all hours. He was sitting up by himself last night in that same chair. He usually slept until almost noon." She paused and her eyes filled again. "I was just—just coming over to see if he was awake, wanting some food."

They looked at each other, without speaking. Hemingway's thoughts raced. What should he do next? Suddenly he realized, even with the woman's apparent acceptance of him, that he'd be under strong suspicion by the police. He, a stranger, discovered bending over a dead body. "Red-handed," they'd call it. He sat down hard in a chair at the table and waited in the silence.

In a few moments, the hall door flew open and Inspector Manot strode into the room followed by Bardon and John Darnell. Manot's gaze flicked about the room, focusing on the body, glancing at Hemingway and at Patricia August. "Stay back. I'll check the body."

Quickly satisfied the man was indeed dead, Manot turned to Hemingway. "You killed this man, didn't you? You'll feel better if you tell me now. Was it for money?"

"No! You're wrong! I didn't kill him. I didn't even know him." Hemingway explained how he came to be in the room and what he and Patricia August had done and said.

"So you ask me to believe you know nothing at all of this murder at your very fingertips?"

Darnell heard the emotion and frustration in Manot's voice. A second killing, the first yet unsolved. He glanced at Bardon and saw in his face the same horror Manot obviously felt, each thinking of reactions of their superiors.

Hemingway answered Manot once more. "I know nothing of it. It was an appointment Mrs. Shelby arranged. I know her daughter, Mary Minter." He gestured at Darnell. "I also know this gentleman. We met in the corridor two nights ago, when I saw what you call the 'ghost' around here. I'm a hotel guest, room 901."

Darnell nodded as Manot turned to him. "Yes, this is the young man, the soldier I told you about. Whatever he is doing here, I don't believe his late arrival at the hotel, well after the first murder, makes him a suspect."

Hemingway said, "Thank you, Professor."

Manot grunted. "Perhaps. We will see." He turned to Patricia August. "You found this man bending over Martin Prince's body?"

"Yes. I came to see Martin as I do about this time."

"You had not spoken to him all morning?"

"No. We talked over champagne last night. I went to my room and read. This morning I ordered breakfast to my room at ten. After that, I must have napped again. When I woke, it was late, and I came over. Martin slept late, but I hadn't heard from him, and I thought he'd want lunch. One of the little things I'd do for him."

Hemingway had taken a small pad and pencil from a pocket and was taking furious notes.

Darnell said, "Shall we search for the weapon, Inspector? It's looks like a garrote again."

Manot nodded. He looked over the area surrounding the chair and the body. "No garrote. No weapon of any kind. Nothing." He noticed an empty champagne bottle and tall glasses on the bar. "My men will inspect the room more carefully."

He turned to Patricia August. "Go to your room, please. Stay there. We will obtain a statement from you later."

After she left the room, Manot said, "I'll get some men out to help."

Bardon groaned. "Two murders. This is ruin! I have to tell the Chairman."

Manot scowled, picked up the phone, and said, "And I must inform Chief Inspector Guerin."

Manot's officers arrived within a half hour. He assigned one officer to accompany Bardon to interview all the ninth-floor staff immediately to determine what any of them might know about anyone entering Prince's suite that morning or the night before. The second officer Manot assigned to inspect the rooms. "Look for a garrotelike instrument—a strip of leather, wire, a cord."

Hemingway brashly continued calling himself a journalist. While Manot was busy, he told Darnell of his desire to be kept in the story, that he'd met Darnell's wife and expressed interest in talking to him.

Darnell admired the young man's energy, with his severe war wounds, and remembered his own eagerness at that age. "I'll speak to the Inspector," he said. "But make yourself invisible. Sit at the table, make your notes. Don't say a word."

Hemingway did exactly that, as Darnell stepped over and spoke to Manot. "He's a witness. Could be valuable later."

Manot grumbled, but with the medical examiner arriving to inspect the body and take notes, preparatory to removing it to the morgue, and the searching of the room in process, he simply waved a hand. "He's your responsibility, then. Just keep him out of the way."

As the medical examiner was finishing his work, Darnell stepped over and observed him and Manot. "Find anything?"

"No, *m'sieur*," the doctor said. "A dead man, strangled with a strong cord. We will examine him further later."

Manot said, "A pen and a hotel envelope in his pocket. Nothing more."

After Inspector Manot's men completed their investigations of the scene with no results, Manot told Darnell, "I must get written statements from Miss August and your soldier."

"You won't need me for that, Louis. I have something else I must do just now."

Chapter Thirteen

Saturday afternoon, December 28

John Darnell took the elevator down to the main
floor. He walked rapidly across the lobby and out
onto the wide walkway of the Champs-Elysees.
Looking one way, then another, he saw the Arc de
Triomphe. He took a deep breath of the fresh air of
Paris, the first he'd had since arriving, and began
walking toward the Arc.

He realized he missed his activities in London,
having been confined for two days in the hotel—his
daily walks about the London streets, whether in sun
or fog or, with umbrella, in the rain. "Prowling," he
called it, and it cleared the brain when he had a
troublesome case. It was that instinct that propelled
him out onto the streets of Paris, even as he knew
important work lay ahead in Le Grand Hotel. His
spirit needed rejuvenation.

Although looking full ahead in his walk, his gaze
fixed on the Arc ahead of him, he caught a glimpse
in his peripheral vision of a face he knew. The man
was walking in the opposite direction, toward the
hotel, his eyes focused on something he carried in
his hand, and clearly not seeing Darnell. Darnell took
a few steps forward, stopped, and turned to peer at

the retreating back of the man. Adrian. The rain chose this moment to begin. Darnell walked on, first in a light drizzle, not a problem for him, with his coat collar turned up. But it soon became a heavy downpour.

When he came upon a small café with a few tables outside under an awning and others inside a glassed-in wall, he ducked under the awning, pulled open the door, and stepped inside. He brushed rain from his coat and with a handkerchief smoothed back his hair.

A moustached maître d' stepped up to him. *"Table, m'sieur?"*

Darnell smiled. "Do you speak English?"

"But, yes."

"A table please, and some coffee. A pot."

"A pot, *m'sieur?*"

"Yes. I need more than your Paris cups hold. It's good, but not enough for an Englishman."

The maître d' smiled and nodded. "You regard them as a *demitasse*. I understand."

Darnell took a seat at a table the man offered, near the window. He'd found at Armand's that ordering a pot of coffee was a solution more suitable than ordering four or five refills.

Waiting for his coffee, he felt an object in his pocket and recalled it was Eric Thorndyke's journal, which he'd taken from the room. He took it out and examined it more closely now. A red, leather-bound journal about half the size of a large hardcover book and only a third as thick, it was a perfect size for portability in a man's pocket, and for inscribing notes. He imagined writers carried such notebooks, and, of course, he did as well, sometimes, on a case.

He cracked the notebook open to the first page, to what Thorndyke apparently considered his title page, and read the words scrawled in large letters in a deliberate hand in the center of it:

A TALKING SCRIPT
NOTES LEADING TO THE DRAFT

Darnell mouthed the words silently—*a talking script*—and shook his head. This was going to be deep waters for him. What did it mean? He paused in his inspection to receive the coffee cup and pot from the waiter, who gave him a condescending look. He poured the cup full and drank the coffee black, half of it, and filled it again from the pot. *What luxury!* He smiled at a local at the next table who seemed fascinated by his procedure.

Back to the journal, Darnell turned pages quickly to get the feel of the note taking. Entries were dated, and they spanned two years. Some jottings were but a few words, others a paragraph or two, all in the same hand. Less than a hundred pages, he estimated. He decided to read a few of the entries, and he could examine the rest later. He drank more coffee as he read page one:

January 1917.
What might be a great idea. Someday motion pictures will have sound. Write a script with actual dialogue for each actor and actress, not the mere mouthing of nothing, nonsense words as they do now. Make it so real and true that when the talking pictures come it could be used for the script—for their lines.

Darnell smiled, with some realization of what the man meant, although he felt it was very premature.

He flipped pages, reading some lines here and there. He was surprised to see it was a tragic love story, the eternal triangle, but not surprised it was set in London, where Thorndyke lived. England was always a good setting for a novel or motion picture. He wondered, did all authors base their stories on their own lives?

He glanced at his watch, and turned to the last entry in the journal:

> *November 20, 1918.*
> *It's finished! And I'll take it to Paris. A classic, I know it is. Must keep it under wraps. He'll want it. I know it. Or—maybe the actress. But it won't be cheap.*

Darnell finished another cup of coffee, left some francs on the table, nodded at the waiter who walked toward him saying, *"Bonsoir, m'sieur,"* and he stepped out onto the windswept, wet walkway. The light vestiges of rain that blew down the Champs-Elysees were reminders of the quick storm that had passed.

As he walked, invigorated now, and with a new purpose—to find that peculiar script and learn more than the journal would disclose—he was eager to return to the investigation.

He'd see Philip Thorndyke and maybe Mary Miles Minter and ask what they knew and thought about the script. He was beginning to feel it played a larger role in the mystery than just another work of fiction. A bit of a passage, one of the early lines he read as he casually glanced at the pages, stood out in his thoughts: *"Good part in this Londontown epic for a young, beautiful actress, sweet young thing. Someone like Pickford, Normand, or M.M.M."*

Upon reaching Le Grand Hotel, John Darnell took another deep breath of the now crisp, rain-fresh air. He entered and strode across the lobby to the elevators. On the ninth floor, he went straight to Martin Prince's room. He found one uniformed officer guarding the door, and with his limited French and the officer's light knowledge of English, he learned Manot had taken written statements from Patricia August and Hemingway, and had gone with the medical examiner and Prince's body to the morgue.

Knowing Penny would not return for another hour or two, he wanted to see the actress and Philip Thorndyke. He stopped at Mary Miles Minter's room and learned from her mother that Mary had accompanied Penny and others for an outing. After knocking on Philip Thorndyke's door persistently, Darnell concluded he, too, had left the hotel.

"Damn!" he said. "This place is like a morgue itself."

As he stood at his own room, about to unlock the door, he saw Philip Thorndyke coming down the hall from the elevator, and he put away his key. In a moment, Thorndyke had reached him.

"May we have a few words, Mr. Thorndyke?"

Philip's eyes met his. "I feel better now. Had a good walk on the boulevard. Afraid I was a bit abrupt earlier." He opened the door to his suite and motioned Darnell to enter.

Thorndyke pointed to the chairs and sofa, and excused himself for a minute or two, going into his bedroom.

Darnell stepped over to the window and gazed out at the panorama of Paris, the sun still obscured by gray clouds, and the lengthening of the afternoon hours becoming apparent in the diminished light. He could see they were in for more rain. He wondered if Penny and her party also had been caught in the early downpour.

Thorndyke reentered the living room and sank into the sofa as Darnell walked back and took a seat opposite him. "You wanted to talk."

"Yes." Darnell pulled out Eric Thorndyke's notebook and held it up between them, noticing Philip's eyebrows raise. "I've read your father's notes, and I know about his so-called talking script now. Why didn't you tell us about it?"

Thorndyke said, "I didn't think it was that important."

"You've read it?"

"No."

"Then . . ."

Thorndyke tensed. "I—I, well, he told me about it, and I thought it was crazy. He always had these ideas. Maybe ahead of his time, I don't know. He was always thinking ahead. But a script for talking pictures?"

"There are such pictures, aren't there? I've heard of some work by De Forest."

Thorndyke nodded. "There have been limited means for sound motion pictures for a dozen years. Phonograph records played at the same time as the picture. Short ones of course, just minutes, and they couldn't synchronize them. The records had deficiencies, cracks sometimes, and in a large room, they weren't loud enough."

"But De Forest . . . ?"

"Yes, he's done some work. My father talked about him. Lee De Forest. He was able to amplify the sound. They used the idea during the war for long-distance radio communications by relays."

"And the synchronization?"

"I'm no technician." He frowned. "My father just said De Forest didn't think much of the phonograph system, which was disjointed and often not in time with the film, and was working on some other method dealing with the sound waves."

"To eliminate the need for a phonograph."

"Yes. To record the sound directly on the film . . . if you can believe that."

"Your father evidently did."

"The public isn't ready for sound films."

"That's your opinion?"

"Well, yes. But even my father admitted that. He knew it was a few years away."

"But he wrote a talking script, as he called it."

"I wish now I'd read it. It's gone."

Darnell looked directly into the other's eyes. "You have no idea where it is?"

"I—I think it's been stolen. Maybe whoever killed my father—"

"Took it."

"Yes."

The young man's glum expression seemed sincere enough to Darnell, and he accepted the man's statements at face value. He'd believe him, for now.

"What do you think about the practicality of the idea?"

Thorndyke raised both hands in the air. "As I said, my father seemed to be at the edge of new ideas, some good ones, some that were doomed. But I think the time for a talking film is still some years away.

I'd say, ten years, but my father would say two or three. He was a dreamer, or an optimist. I don't know which." He paused. "I'd been away from him for a while."

Darnell nodded. "From what I've read of your father's notes, he seemed positive about the script's value. He had a story line, and even had names picked out for possible stars of the picture. We have to find that script, Philip."

Thorndyke shook his head. "That would be your job, to find it, wouldn't it? Or the Inspector's. What—search the hotel?"

"It could easily have been removed from this room and from the hotel, even the same night. It could be anywhere."

Thorndyke sighed. "There are some things I'd better tell you." He seemed to gather his thoughts or determination. "At least two people here want that script. They've approached me. The Dutch woman, Edda Van Eych, came to me asking about my father's secret work. She seemed to know something about it, but didn't use the word 'script.' I think she thought it was a book."

"And the other?"

"Charlotte Shelby. The mother of the actress. A very savvy woman. She knew it was a script. Maybe her daughter told her, because I saw my father talking with the girl, pawing her, at the party. Probably told her about it."

"How much did Mrs. Shelby know about it?"

"I don't think she'd read it, but she knew it had a part in it for a young girl like her daughter. I expect my father told Mary Minter about that—for his own reasons. Mrs. Shelby wanted to buy it, looked dejected when I told her I didn't have it. I imagine she'd consider it a coup to have her daughter in the first big talking movie."

Darnell thought a bit. "What do the actors and actresses say to each other now when the silent cameras film them?"

Philip Thorndyke laughed, the first time Darnell could recall the man showing any humor. "You'd be surprised. The director doesn't tell them what to say. There is no script of words. There's just an idea for the film, and notes about the action. The director imagines the rest. No rehearsal, not like a stage play. They put on clothes from wardrobe, take positions, do the actions, move their lips, saying whatever they want. The language sometimes—well, it's very bald. The directors don't care. They think it spices up the emotions and the film."

"A talking script, as your father termed it, would give each actor specific lines, line for line, for each scene."

"Exactly. In a silent film, even now, it would add to the realism. The viewer could see some of the words match the screen titles. But I think he was planning ahead for the first talking moving picture. I knew him that well. He wanted to be first."

"Now you could become famous with that script— with the first talking picture."

Philip Thorndyke nodded. "Maybe I could."

Chapter Fourteen

Saturday evening, December 28

Penny Darnell finished freshening up after the outing. She felt invigorated enough to talk with John, now, when he returned. They hadn't had much time when his mind wasn't on the crime. How would she approach it? He should be relaxed. A bit of sherry? As she found the bottle and glasses, she heard a key rattling in the door and he entered. She could see at once something new had happened, and that this was no time for family talk.

"There's been another killing," John Darnell said, taking her into his arms.

Her expression changed from the glow of excitement at her day's experiences to one of alarm. "Oh, no! Who was it, John?"

"Martin Prince."

She held him tightly for a moment, then sat on the bed and shook her head, reorganizing her thoughts. "How did it happen?" She kicked off her shoes.

He sat next to her and explained, not too graphically, how Prince had died by another apparent garroting, and that his body had been taken to the morgue.

"How gruesome." She looked at him. "That makes it a harder case for you, doesn't it? Two killings, now."

"More complicated in one way, maybe simpler in another."

"Simpler?"

"I mentioned to Manot that the murder of Eric Thorndyke might have been a mistake, that someone may have mistook him for Prince, and he liked that idea. Certainly there were motives enough against Prince, and now he's dead. But now I'm having second thoughts. Still, if it isn't that, the two deaths are connected in some way we don't know yet."

"Who found him—I mean, the body?"

"The soldier, Hemingway."

"But he had breakfast with us and went off with Mary."

"He came back, went to Prince's room . . ."

She frowned. "I want you to be careful, John. It seems the police can't prevent a murder right here on our own floor."

"To do that, they'd have to post an officer at every door."

She stood up and walked to the closet. "Maybe they should. The women in the group must be afraid of what could happen next."

"I think I've disposed of the ghost matter, once and for all."

"Oh, really?"

"He denies it, but I'm sure it was Adrian the Magician, dressed up in Thorndyke's clothes. I think Philip Thorndyke put him up to it to flush out his father's killer, or as a smoke screen."

"Meaning?"

"A smoke screen—if one of them is actually the murderer."

Penny frowned. "You always talk about motive

and psychology as being so important. What possible motive could the magicin have?"

"Money is one. I'm just not dropping him from the suspect list. I believe some of these people more than others, but there is still deception out there."

"Any other clues?" She smiled. "Anything I can help you with?"

"With this," he said, and kissed her again, holding her longer this time. When the telephone rang, Darnell picked up the receiver with a free hand, said a word, listened, and hung up.

"Good or bad news?" she asked.

"I don't know. It's just that Inspector Manot's back. He wants me in the lobby." He stood next to her and pulled her close. "You have to be very careful, too. Don't be alone with just one person at any time, because we don't know who the killer could be. There's safety in numbers. Two or more."

She nodded. "You'll be back up for dinner?"

"After I talk with Manot, I'll call you."

"All right, John. I have some things to do here." She kissed him.

"Put the second latch on," he said, as he stepped through the doorway and pulled the door closed behind him.

She latched it and sat down on the bed, glum. Another opportunity to talk lost. She sighed. She knew John would be preoccupied until all the loose ends were tied together and the killer identified. Time enough then.

Darnell waited until he heard the latch close, then walked to the elevator. As he rode down to the lobby, he thought of another possibility he'd talk with Penny about later—he could send her back to London, where it was safe. One murder before they arrived was one thing. A second, a few doors away, another.

Inspector Manot rose from his chair in the lobby as he saw John Darnell approach from the elevator area. Two officers who flanked Manot on adjacent chairs at the table rose also, but he motioned them down. For the second time in the case, Louis Manot felt he could lose this one. If so, it would be the first he hadn't solved since making Inspector six years ago. But such a high-profile case could hurt his chances to become Chief Inspector, perhaps to succeed Guerin when he retired in a few years. Stymied and edgy, he hoped Darnell, who had shown some insight and had effectively identified the ghost, could help solve these real-world murders. He was glad Darnell was in it.

He held a hand out to Darnell who shook it and moved right into the vitals of the inquiry. "Bring me up to date, Louis. You took statements? An autopsy has begun?"

"Have a seat here, John. These are Officers Vardan and Roche." The officers and Darnell exchanged nods, and Darnell looked expectantly at Manot. Louis Manot glanced about the room. No one nearby, although a constant flow of hotel guests moved about, some hurrying in one direction, others the opposite.

"The preliminary autopsy tests and observations of the medical examiner show that the rigor mortis was complete. That means it was at least eight to twelve hours earlier that Prince was killed. That would put it between midnight and four this morning. With body temperature considered, the ME believes midnight to two most likely."

"Any other aspects?"

Manot shook his head. "As you know, the eyes were open, the jaw dropped open too. That's normal. His coloring shows the body had been in the position in which it was found—in the chair. The feet, you know, and his backside—dark gray-blue."

"Murdered just as he sat."

"*Exactement*."

"By someone he knew, of course."

Manot said, "Yes. He must have opened the door to that person, then resumed his seat while the other had freedom of the room—to move about, take a position behind him, apply the garrote to his unsuspecting neck."

"Anything else?"

"They will do the usual tests. But I expect nothing more interesting, no poison or other contributing cause of death."

"Your statements from Patricia August and the soldier?"

"Merely repeated what they said. But the time of death rules out Hemingway, at least as to today's situation."

Darnell nodded. "If the body had complete rigor, Hemingway had nothing to do with it. Prince had been dead for hours."

Manot ran a hand through his hair, which he felt, quite irrationally, had taken on more gray since he woke that morning. "I need something to tell my Chief. I see him in the morning."

Manot listened with widening eyes as Darnell told of Eric Thorndyke's notes describing the talking script, and what Philip had said about it. *This could be it*, Manot thought—*the breakthrough I need. "Voilà!"*

he said. "Whoever killed Thorndyke murdered him to get it. We must find the script."

Darnell frowned. "Not so easy at this point. But why would Prince be murdered over the script?"

Manot recoiled. "Well, maybe to take the script from him. Yes—Prince had it, and the killer took it. It has value." He smiled. He knew that would satisfy Guerin as a new line of inquiry. He looked at Darnell with a sense of satisfaction. Now all they had to do was find it. But Darnell's words stuck in his mind. *Not so easy.*

Ernest Hemingway ignored the patrons in the brasserie as he put his arm around Mary Miles Minter. Damn the busybodies! "Let's find a booth where we can talk," he said. He took her hand and walked, cane in the other, to the last booth. They sat in it, side by side.

"You said they suspected you after you found the body?"

He nodded. "My career could be over before it begins. 'Kansas City Star *reporter at murder scene.*' Oh, they'll be careful—they can't call me a suspected murderer and get away with it. They don't want to be sued. And I think by now they probably know I didn't do it."

"The police haven't taken you in. They must feel you're innocent."

When the waiter came, Hemingway ordered a beer for himself and a soft drink for her. "Can you imagine walking in on that scene?"

Her eyes softened under his gaze. "Yes. Remember, I saw Mr. Thorndyke's body, you know, at the party. We all did."

"They must be connected—two murders in the same group."

"Now you're thinking like a reporter. You could do your own investigation, and write an exclusive story."

"I've already started. I talked with Miss August. I was in the room while they were poking about. Got some good notes. I had to sign a statement, but I learned a bit more then." He drained half the beer mug the waiter brought. "It's an article, now; I know I can do that. But I can also use some of this in a book someday. Like how Prince's face looked in death." He drank some more. "I've seen violent deaths on the battlefield, that's not new for me. But confronting it in a luxury hotel like this—it's different. It makes you think no place is safe."

"You're right. It's make-believe up on the screen in Hollywood, but in the real town, even the stars and directors lead real lives. A lot of things go on there. Bad things. Crime. Even killings."

He smiled now at her serious face. "All right. I worried too much. But I'm glad I have you to hear me out. Advice from a girl in her teens. Just what a soldier needs."

She looked at him with the blue eyes that bothered him so. "I know more about life than you'd expect, Ernest Hemingway. Life in Hollywood grows you up very fast."

With the security chain still on the door, Trisha August opened her door a crack in answer to the knock. Cynthia Fitch stood in the hallway.

Cynthia said, "I thought you could use some company."

Trisha realized the woman was right about that—

but this woman? The wife of the man she hoped someday to marry?

"I—I don't know." She stared at her.

"Some of us are meeting in the lounge next to Armand's restaurant—just the women, you understand. For a cocktail. I've spoken with Sylvia Beach, Edda Van Eych, and Charlotte Shelby. They're there already. The young girl is busy."

Trisha considered. In a group, she could tolerate being in the same environment as Cynthia Fitch without embarrassment.

"We'll stop and pick up the Professor's wife, too," Cynthia was saying.

Trisha sighed. "All right." She closed the door, removed the chain, and opened it again. "Come in for a minute. I'll just freshen up."

She stepped into her bedroom and the adjoining bathroom, allowing Mrs. Fitch—how she hated that word, "Mrs."—to close the door and fend for herself. Five minutes later she walked back out in a different dress, with a bit of makeup on, and her hair brushed out, smoother, tidier. She did feel better, doing just that much.

They went on to the Darnells' room, and after some persuasion, the two of them prevailed on Penny to join them. She too freshened her appearance, then wrote a short note to her husband and placed it prominently on the table. "Have to keep John informed where I am. Worries, if I don't."

The three rode down the elevator to the mezzanine and soon greeted the others and took seats at the large window table in the cocktail lounge. Trisha realized at once that the others wanted to hear about the crime from her—she had seen Prince's dead body.

After they all ordered drinks and began sipping them, Sylvia Beach said, "It's all over the hotel. Word of these things travels fast."

Edda Van Eych asked hesitantly, "Another strangling? The garotte?" It seemed to Trisha the woman was more interested in the method than the man.

"What does it matter? He's gone," Trisha said. "You don't know this, but I worked with Martin for eleven years. Began as a junior, worked my way up the ladder." She gave them a rueful smile. "Funny, you know—he was talking about the top of that ladder, where he was, just the night before. Said it was shaky, and sometimes someone down there was doing the shaking, trying to tumble you off."

"Do you have any idea why he was killed?" asked Cynthia Fitch.

Suddenly she remembered her time with David Fitch just before he met with Martin Prince, and the angry words that filtered through the walls from Prince's room to her own when the two men met. *Shaky ladder*. That worry could have come to Martin from David, from what he said. This was dangerous territory. She could not inadvertently implicate David.

She took a breath and at last answered the question. "No. Nothing at all."

"Whoever murdered Eric Thorndyke killed your employer," Edda Van Eych said. "Does anyone disagree with that?" She glared about the table, challenging them to argue the point, but they shook their heads and said nothing. She went on. "I think I know something about all this."

Trisha looked at her, but bit her lip and said nothing, waiting. She looked from one face to another, but saw nothing there to reveal any sign of guilty knowledge, only curiosity and fascination with a crime so close to their own lives. In a macabre way, she sensed that if Martin were here he would be reveling in such an atmosphere of intrigue, thinking of the book possibilities. Was he up there—somewhere—rubbing his hands together as he did when he found a new book, urging her on to get a meeting going? Silly thoughts! She shook her head in disgust at her own musings, and came into the middle of what the Van Eych woman was saying.

". . . When Eric talked with me, I had the feeling he had a secret, something that could be worth a lot of money. I don't know what it was. But"—she paused, obviously for dramatic effect—"maybe it was a book."

"But if it was a book . . . ," Trisha began.

". . . He would have shown it to Mr. Prince," Edda said.

Sylvia Beach said, "Two men murdered for a book? I'd like to put *that* book on display in my store."

Trisha turned to Penny. "What does your husband think? Can he tell us anything? We deserve to know."

"He's meeting with the Inspector. They have their methods. And John would not be hasty in reaching conclusions. He's very thorough."

Trisha again thought of David. She was the only one who knew of his argument with Martin. She had to keep the Professor away from that idea at all costs.

Addressing them all, Trisha said, "We need to look out for each other, protect each other. So far, it's two men who have been murdered. But with a *maniac*— that's who I think the killer is—any one of us could be next."

"We stick together, then," Edda said. She scowled at the other women. "But I still think a book was involved."

Let them believe that, Trisha thought, as the women stood and said good nights. Watching Charlotte Shelby walk ahead of her, she realized Charlotte was the only one who said nothing about the murder, or the book. Not one word.

Activities during the remainder of the evening reflected the depressing atmosphere outside, the ominous dark rain clouds over Paris. All in the Prince entourage seemed to change their plans after hearing of the murder.

Manot called on all of them, asking whether they had any information on the murder, reviewing their previous night's activities. Hemingway, eager earlier to see the Folies Bergere, told Mary Minter he would stay in his room and do some writing, or try to seek out Manot or Darnell for information.

Manot found Mary Miles Minter and her mother dining in their own room. Trisha August told Manot she had no appetite when he stopped by, and seemed to be drinking a liquid dinner in the form of French white wine. Edda Van Eych informed him she would work on her own book in her room.

When Manot stopped at the Spaniard's room, he saw Camilo had ordered up two bottles of red wine. Later he found Ward with Tyler spending the evening talking and drinking in the brasserie. Manot spoke with Sylvia Beach as she left the hotel to eat at a nearby local restaurant on her way back to her apartment. He stopped at Armand's, noticing the Fitches dining there as he walked to the table where

John Darnell and Penny sat. With a sigh, he informed Darnell of his fruitless inquiries. They were all keeping to themselves, concerned, watchful and separate, and none of their activities would intersect that night.

Although Darnell felt certain Adrian would never again masquerade as a ghost, just to prove it to himself, he spent a lonely forty minutes in the same ninth-floor corridor alcove. He saw nothing, and crawled into bed next to a sleeping Penny, at half past twelve.

Chapter Fifteen

Sunday morning, December 29

John and Penny Darnell began the day having breakfast in their room, enjoying the small comfort of hot coffee as they stared out at the driving rain spattering against their windows.

He looked across the table at Penny. "So—the women have formed their own little protection society?"

She sniffed. "Don't laugh. As I told you last night, John, underneath, they're very concerned. They're scared, and with good reason. They asked me what you're doing to solve this."

"And you told them . . . ?"

"That you're very thorough, dear." Penny smiled. "That I don't know everything that goes on in your mind."

"But you do know the important things there." He reached across the table, pulled her closer to him, and kissed her. "Like this."

She sighed, and glanced at a clock. "We have so little time alone. What are your plans today?"

He regarded her with serious eyes, and decided this would be the time to ask her his question.

"Something I wanted to talk with you about. What would you think of going back to London?"

"What?"

"For your safety. Two murders . . ."

Penny's eyes flashed. "John, you knew about one of those before we even came over here. And I'm in no more danger than any of those other women." She softened a bit, remembering her own thoughts over the past three days. "I know your work involves danger—these murderous situations. Sometimes, well, I feel like Ulysses' wife. Her name was Penelope, too. The difference is, she stayed home, while he went on his adventures. I go with you. I knew about your cases when I married you, John, and that's part of my life. You're my life." She took a breath. "No. I'm staying right here with you."

Darnell put his arm around her shoulders. "All right, all right. I had to ask. Calm down—my Penelope."

She sighed. "Okay." She smiled at him. "Now where were we?"

"You asked what I was going to do today."

"And?"

"Another visit to the *Sûreté* headquarters this morning. Manot said he'd pick me up at ten." He checked the time. "I suppose I'd better get ready."

"If you must, then." She sat back and looked at him silently. She laid a hand on his.

"Manot said he'd call first." Darnell smiled. "When he does, I'll tell him—make it eleven."

Trisha August watched through the crack in her door, slightly ajar, as the man moved quickly across the corridor. She swung the door open wide. David Fitch entered the room, swiftly but without noise closed the door, and stepped into her welcoming arms.

"I'm glad you could come," Trisha said, and studied his face for the instant before he kissed her. Eyes closed, she kissed him, but the image of his face glowed in her mind. What was she looking for there? Guilt? Can you read it on a man's face?

In a moment, she felt him relax in her arms.

He still held her. "You've been through a lot," he said.

She broke free, stepped over to the table, took a cigarette from a pack, and lit it. She blew smoke into the air and sat on the sofa.

He walked over and sat next to her, arm around her shoulders. "Prince's death complicates things," Fitch said.

She nodded. "I'm communicating with my headquarters. After the police finish their inquiries—if they ever do—I'll close down this little soiree and head back to New York."

"And when will I see you?"

She looked into his face again, into his eyes. Could he have done it? She couldn't allow herself to think it. "When? That's up to you, David. You know where I'll be." She paused. "You told me about some of your dreams, last time you were here. Before you . . . saw Prince." She watched his expression. Not a flicker.

"Dreams can come true. We'll be in that small hotel overlooking the ocean someday. I'm studying something important that could speed it up."

"Your divorce?"

"Eventually. But more to the point, acquiring control over American-Universal Publishing Company. My advisors tell me it can be done without costing a fortune."

She gave him a wry smile. "Since when have you been worried about spending a fortune? You have several of them."

"I'm not used to wealth, yet. The war made me wealthy. I'm sorry to say that, but it's true."

"But there's a difference. You're not sorry that it's true."

He looked at her. "Have I done something? You're rather sharp with me."

She softened, and stroked his cheek, and impulsively kissed him. "It's just—I don't know what to think. This murder . . ."

"Prince's murder. You don't think—you know I wouldn't have done that." He pulled back from her, and she could feel his intense gaze. "I'm no killer."

"You wanted to acquire the company . . . and you wanted me. Just tell me you didn't do it, David. Tell me that." She took one of his hands in both of hers.

Fitch broke her light hold on him and stood. "I know it may look suspicious. You probably heard us arguing, is that it?"

Trisha nodded. "The walls are thin."

"I see now. But I swear it was not me."

Trisha stood close to him and allowed him to take her in his arms again and kiss her. But her eyes were open this time, and a deep frown creased her forehead.

Bert Ward looked across the brasserie table at Brandon Tyler. The publisher had urged him to join him in some drinks again, saying they never really touched on anything important the night before.

"Important?" Ward repeated. "Isn't a murder important?"

"Certainly. But we talked that to death yesterday. I think it was the Spaniard, probably said as much after a few drinks."

Ward shrugged. "I'm willing to forget all that."

The waiter brought mugs of beer and each of them drank large swallows. Ward eyed the other. "So, what is important, then?"

Tyler studied Ward's face. "You're close to Fitch, aren't you? In on some of his schemes, aware of his plans? That information could be valuable to me. That's what's important."

Ward sipped his beer, watching Tyler. This could be turned to his advantage, if he played it smart. "Well, yes and no. I might be."

"Might be, if the price were right, is that it?"

"I don't like to go out too far on a limb. It could get sawed off. What's on your mind?" He sat back and waited. Tyler would get to it in his conservative, businessman roundabout way.

"I have heard from friends and associates that David Fitch may take a financial interest in American-Universal Publishing. I don't mean a token interest. A big one. That could be important to me. I have the publishing and distribution rights in England for their books. But the contract can be cancelled."

Ward smiled. "I heard Prince might have done that himself. Not a bad motive for murder."

Tyler flinched. "Don't even say that in jest, Ward. I would never have killed a man just over a contract."

"Just for millions of pounds?" Ward smirked. "No, of course not. Forgive me for mentioning it."

"Dammit, man!" Tyler drained his beer mug and motioned to the waiter for two more. "You're not funny, not at all, and don't be passing those remarks on to others."

"You mean, to Inspector Manot?" Ward lifted his hands as if to say he couldn't help himself. And, in fact, he was enjoying irritating the man. Maybe the price would go up now.

"Enough. Now listen, I'm willing to pay for information, but not this kind of rot. What have you heard from Fitch about his plans to buy into the company? That could be worth something to you."

Ward finished his mug, pushed it aside, and began on the new one. "I would say, roughly, it could be worth a thousand pounds. And that's roughly. Depends on what I have to do."

Tyler said nothing for a moment, drinking, and Ward could see thoughts flying across the man's face. Calculations.

"All right," Tyler said, looking directly into Ward's eyes. "You named your price. I'll pay it if you really have solid information."

Ward's mouth screwed up and his eyes narrowed. "And a good-faith payment, a down payment, if you will?"

Tyler scowled, but reached for his wallet in his inside coat pocket. He held it down below the table level, out of Ward's sight, and Ward heard the rustling of bills.

"Here's two hundred pounds. If your information is good, in my judgment, I'll pay you the rest. If it isn't, you keep the two hundred against a project of trying again. Then you'll get the rest."

Ward nodded. "Fair enough." He took the bills from him and tucked them into his pocket.

"I'll get you what you need. Here's a little preview."

Tyler said nothing, waited, and drank greedily of his beer. He kept his gaze fixed on Ward.

"Fitch has been having this running conversation in London at his club, at his home over the phone, with his cronies. He's talking of taking over American-Universal Publishing Company, but he wants others to front for him. He'll put up the money. That he has. But he doesn't want his role to be public."

"All right, he's shy. But does he have a deal yet? What he does could affect me, and I'd want to talk with him while we're here. And is he going to do it?"

Ward said, "Yes, but the deal may not be set in concrete yet. I'll keep my ears open. I'm convinced of it so far from everything I've heard. Anyway, you'd be safe in talking with him, making your pitch."

Tyler relaxed, smiled. He wiped a touch of perspiration from his forehead with a napkin. "Well, I guess you're closer to that other eight hundred."

Ward grinned. "Do you have it with you? We could settle it right now."

Tyler shook his head. "I'll need more than what you've got so far. And I'll talk with Fitch. If I come away feeling you were right, you'll get it, whether or not I'm successful with him. I'm a man of my word."

Edda Van Eych rested her head on Ricardo Camilo's shoulder in the bed in his room. After they shared a bottle of red wine, and with thunder and lightning and the heavy, lulling rain outside, they soon found themselves in each other's arms and in the dark.

"I do love you, Ricardo." She liked the feeling of his strong body lying next to her, and it took her out of herself, away from the deep subjects that racked her mind these past days in this hotel. She knew she must look out for herself, as all the others were evidently doing, avoid suspicion, get through it. But she worried about Camilo. "Yes, I love you. But you lie, you get drunk—I think you're on the edge of danger."

"You are a lovely lady, but you worry too much," he answered, not the words she wanted to hear, but they would have to do.

"The police have talked to you?" She turned her head to look at him.

"Always, they talk. Do they ask about Prince? Yes."

"What do they say?"

"They dare not accuse me. They have no evidence. I am innocent."

Edda smiled. "Strange choice of words. You may not be guilty, but I think you are not innocent."

Camilo frowned. "What is the difference?"

"It is a language subtlety. I am not English either. I am . . . Dutch." She frowned, but went on. "*Innocent* means pure. *Not guilty* means they did not prove you committed a crime."

"I am not pure?" He pulled her to him.

She said, "Not sinless, not unblemished. But as far as my loving you is concerned, with no flaw."

He looked at her. "You're confusing me. Then am I guilty? Of the crime of killing Prince?"

She stared at the ceiling. "I only tease you, my lover. Now that I've been in your arms, I do not think you could have killed him. Or anyone."

"I think the *Sûreté* does."

"I talk to you about all this because, well, I have a secret, too. It is time for me to tell someone."

He looked at her and smiled. "You're a murderer?"

"No. I am German. My father opposed the war there and was killed. I fled Germany for my life and pretended to be Dutch."

Camilo took her hand. "It doesn't matter. One day we'll be in Spain together and we will forget all of the past. And the war."

Chapter Sixteen

Sunday morning, December 29

John Darnell stood in front of Le Grand Hotel on the Champs-Elysees watching for Manot's car. He glanced at his pocket watch. Eleven-fifteen a.m., now past the agreed time of eleven.

Looking at the watch, he smiled wryly, thinking of when he'd looked at it on the upturned lifeboat after the *Titanic* sank, seeing the watch stopped at 2:20 A.M. It took a watchmaker a week and an entirely new set of workings to put it in operation again, but it was worth it for the constant reminder, the memory, of what he and Penny and his manservant Sung had gone through that night and morning.

The quick sound of a horn caught his attention, and an unmarked gray *Sûreté* car pulled up at the curb. Manot, in the backseat, pushed the door open and said, "Excuse—I am late. Troops coming back held up the traffic. It is nice to see them return, but everything stops. People watch, and wave at them."

Darnell stepped into the car, pulled the door closed, and it drew out into traffic, turning back at the next street and heading in the direction of *Sûreté* headquarters. He looked at Manot, who appeared rested and confident.

"We see Chief Inspector Guerin at noon," Manot said with a lilt in his voice. "We will tell him of the script. . . . What did you call it?"

"A 'MacGuffin.'" Darnell laughed. "It's an old Scottish and English term that has become associated with crime. It means, well, any solid object, sometimes valuable, with special import, that has a direct impact or meaning in a criminal case."

"I see. Yes, it has that, certainly. It may be the key to unraveling these murders. Someone killed two people for it."

Darnell frowned. "That's a good supposition, but we're not sure of it, not all of it. It may be that someone murdered Eric Thorndyke for the script. But how does Prince come into it? Unless he had the script somehow, and someone . . ." He shook his head. "But then that would assume Prince was Thorndyke's killer to get the script and someone else then murdered him? No, I think both murders were done by the same hand."

"By the same hand, yes. Thorndyke could have left the script with Prince to read. Someone could have learned that."

"We do tend to go around in circles on that one. But the important thing is, we have to search the rooms of everyone in Prince's entourage. That may turn up the script, and who knows what else." He nodded, more to himself than Manot. "What we need now from your Chief Inspector is search warrants."

"He resisted them, called it—how do you say— an expedition to fish? There are important people involved that must not be offended. But now we have a second murder and the missing script." Manot set his jaw. "With your help, we'll get them."

Chief Inspector Guerin received Manot and Darnell with energy and interest, sweeping them into his office and closing the door quickly. "What you have found?" He looked at Manot. "Your message sounded urgent."

"It is not what we have found, Chief, it is what we haven't found." As the three seated themselves, Manot went on, "An important motion-picture script is missing."

Guerin frowned. "A script?"

"For the making of a motion picture. Eric Thorndyke, the first victim, had worked on one for months, perhaps years. It was in his room. He was killed, and it disappeared."

"This is the breakthrough you spoke of on the phone?"

"It could be very important."

"It must be, to bring me in here on a Sunday." Guerin looked at Darnell. "What do you think, Professor?"

Darnell had anticipated the question and knew exactly how he wanted to answer it. "We must search all the rooms of all the people who met Prince in the hotel. It may not be too late to find it."

Guerin scowled. "I don't see the importance of this—this, script. They take the camera, shoot the picture, *n'est-ce pas*? Why a script? Why words? We do not hear the actors speak."

Darnell explained the features of what Thorndyke had called the talking script. "Sound is coming to film one day. Thorndyke may have thought it would come sooner than may actually happen. No one knows. He was an optimist. But he had studied the idea carefully, and put a lot of work into it."

"Would this script lead us to the murderer?"

Manot said, "Yes."

Darnell said, "It could. We won't know until we find it."

"It is our only lead," Manot said. "And a good one."

"And you want . . . ?"

Manot looked Guerin in the eye. "The search warrants, Chief Inspector. Nothing less will do it."

Guerin walked to the window and stared out. "Very well. Prepare the papers. I will sign them. You will route them."

"I'll do that. Thank you, Chief."

Guerin turned, stepped over to shake hands with Darnell. "Two days before this year ends. Try to clear this up by then."

Manot and Darnell walked out into the hall and down a few doors to Manot's office. "These papers will take some time," Manot said. "I'll order a car to take you back to Le Grand."

Darnell nodded. "Call me there when you have the papers."

His ride back to the hotel gave Darnell an opportunity to think through some aspects that bothered him. The rain did not lessen, coming down steadily.

As he entered the hotel lobby and walked through it, he looked about the room and saw members of the Prince group sitting, talking, drinking champagne to fill the aimless hours. Some held sway in the brasserie, and he imagined others encamped in the mezzanine cocktail lounge or lingering over a meal at

Armand's. His step quickened as he approached the elevators. He was sure Penny would want lunch now, and he felt suddenly famished. They would find a quiet corner at Armand's.

As afternoon hours lengthened, Edda Van Eych sat in the hotel lobby, staring at a newspaper but not absorbing the words. *That Thorndyke book, or whatever it is!* If she could find it, make it hers, she might get leverage with Patricia August and American-Universal, now that Prince was out of her way. *But, wait—Cynthia Fitch knows of Thorndyke's project.*

Just as the name flickered in her mind, David Fitch strode briskly across the lobby, heading straight for the brasserie. Meeting someone? Probably will have business there, a drink or two. Edda knew the opportunity might not come again for a talk with Cynthia. She tossed down the newspaper and hurried to an elevator. Exiting at the ninth floor, she quickly approached the Fitches' room and rapped on the door, hoping to find Cynthia in.

The door opened, and Cynthia Fitch looked at her with surprise in her eyes. "Edda—you look upset. What is it?"

"Nothing serious. But I am on edge. I just vant to talk. Do you have a few minutes?"

Cynthia hesitated for a moment, puffing on the cigarette she held in her fingers. "Well . . . all right. Come in."

Edda walked past her into the living room and stopped near the sofa. Cynthia closed the door and walked over to her.

Cynthia said, "Let's sit down. What is it, Edda?"

They took seats, and Edda leaned toward Cynthia. "There is something—it could help me a lot, and cost you nothing. Information."

Cynthia Fitch smiled. "Sounds mysterious. Everything in this hotel is, I suppose."

"Remember Prince's big party? Everybody talking?"

"Ye-es?"

"I overheard—forgive me—Eric Thorndyke talking to you."

Cynthia stiffened in her chair, ground out her cigarette in an ashtray, and moved as if to stand. "Eavesdropping on others' conversations?"

"No. Not on purpose. Accidental. I heard something about a special project, and I suppose my ears pricked up at that. His voice carried."

"Oh . . . the special project. Yes, he had a strong voice."

"If I could find that book . . ."

"Book?"

"His project."

"No, Edda, it wasn't a book. It was a movie idea of some kind. I don't know much about that sort of thing. Party talk, in between glasses of champagne, you know."

Edda sat back, feeling sharp disappointment. No book. A setback. She sighed. "All right, I hoped—but forget it." She stood. "I leave now." She held out a stiff hand, which Cynthia shook. She walked to the doorway and out into the hall.

Edda stopped and took a breath. Her own book turned down by Prince. Her idea of taking over Thorndyke's project now apparently dead. She could plead mercy to Patricia August. Or . . . could she tell

Patricia that Prince liked her book? But he may have confided in her. Edda sighed, thought of Camilo, and walked to his door. There would be comfort there.

Brandon Tyler, armed with the information bought from Bert Ward, walked toward the door of the brasserie opening into the hotel lobby, but pulled up short as he saw David Fitch approach.

"Mr. Fitch," Tyler said, standing between him and the entrance to the brasserie.

Fitch's expression took on a note of annoyance and surprise.

"Tyler? What is it, man? I'm in a bit of a hurry."

"Just a few minutes of your time." He gestured toward a table and chairs in the corner of the lobby. "A small private talk."

Fitch made a show of pulling out his watch and looking at it. "Ten minutes? Will that do?"

"Yes, thank you." Tyler felt good about this. Fresh from his talk with Ward he had a new sense of confidence. As the two sat at the table, Tyler searched the other's face for attitude and thought he saw there a spark of interest, or the eternal greed.

"Things have changed drastically in the past twenty-four hours," Tyler began. "Since Martin Prince's death."

Fitch nodded. "I see. You're his London man."

"Exactly. Just what I want to talk with you about. I've been the London man—the English outlet for American-Universal, if you will—for fifteen years now, even before Martin Prince joined them. I'd like to continue in that mode. I've got some ideas, now that the war's over, for boosting sales."

Fitch glanced about the room. No one in the group there. "And why are we sitting here, talking about it, Tyler?"

"I've heard some things—quietly you understand, I never broadcast these matters—that you are considering taking over American-Universal Publishing Company."

Fitch straightened in his chair. "And where—?"

"Please, Mr. Fitch. As I say, it's a quiet thing—a few words here and there in a London club, a private phone call. I've not discussed this with anyone."

Fitch bristled. "Nor would I advise it."

Tyler rushed on. "Here's my point. I want to work with you after the, ah, ownership change. I can be valuable to you in England. You'll have to be in New York some of the time, maybe much of the time, at the headquarters. Watching your money."

"And if this were all true, how would you fit in?"

"I know the publishing business. I know American-Universal. I know my way around in England. And I'd be grateful for the continued connection." His voice lowered. "I would propose that you take a twenty percent—no, twenty-five percent—interest in my firm, your cost to be paid entirely out of future profits. No cash up front. We'd be in the business here together."

Fitch's eyes narrowed. He said, "Your time's up. I have an appointment." He stood and looked at the other. "It might make sense. All right, Tyler. Make up a business plan. Twenty-five percent. We'll talk more about that later, back in London." He grimaced. "If we ever get out of this damned hotel prison."

They shook hands, and Tyler watched David Fitch stride back toward the brasserie. He felt good about it now. Fitch liked the ownership idea, he could see that. He could salvage his business, now that Prince was no longer an obstacle. He sat down again at the table in a sort of reverie, thinking ahead. In a moment, he became aware of a presence.

Bert Ward stood before him, looking down at him. Ward smiled. "You look like the cat that swallowed a canary. And I've been watching. Shall we settle up on that other eight hundred, now? I can see you bloody well got what you wanted from the man."

Chapter Seventeen

Sunday afternoon, December 29

Mary Miles Minter hugged Ernest Hemingway's side, holding on to his arm as they walked down the Champs-Elysees during a lull in the rain. "I missed seeing you last night," she said, looking up at him, watching his expression.

He nodded. "Everyone wanted to hide out after the second murder. I wrote up my notes and observations. It takes a lot of time putting a feature article like that together. At best, it can be like a short story or novella, with suspense and drama."

"So you weren't hiding out from me?"

"No. I almost expected the *Sûreté* to knock on my door at any hour and drag me down to headquarters. But they didn't. I think they've dropped me as a suspect. I saw the Professor meet Inspector Manot out in front of the hotel earlier."

"Ernest . . ."

"I need to see the Professor again. He helped me."

"Why don't you just catch him at lunch or dinner? That's one time he wouldn't be interrogating people, or sniffing about for clues."

He smiled. "You do think about things, don't you? How about this? I think I prefer you call me Ernie, now. In fact, I don't even like Ernest, except maybe on a book cover."

"You should have mentioned it."

"I didn't mind when you said it."

"Okay, then, *Ernie* . . . think about this. We'll be parting company in a few days."

He nodded. "I know. I have to leave the day after New Year's to return to Italy and catch my ship. I'll go to America from Genoa."

"Floating out of my life."

He fell silent for a moment. "There was a woman I met in Italy—a nurse. I want you to know that."

She tossed her curls back. "There's always a somebody somewhere. There's William back in Hollywood—but I don't know if I really want to see him again. Except when he directs me. And you may never ever see your—your nurse." Her voice broke.

"It's true. We'll never see each other. I had to tell you so I could put it behind me. All I want to do now is write."

"So you'll write. About the war, you said. Your adventures in the war, maybe."

"Not my adventures, particularly." Hemingway laughed. "Driving an ambulance, taking chocolates to troops. I did get a dose of shrapnel—and it almost ruined my legs. But I wasn't any hero, really. I couldn't sleep for a long time afterward without a light on. But it gave me a feeling of what war is all about. It's the best subject to write about—the fear, the action, the agony. Yes, war, and now that I've seen it here, murder." He paused. "And, of course, love."

"And what about us?"

"When I tell my family I met you, a motion-picture star, they won't believe a word of it. I tell some fanciful tales. They call it lying. I call it telling stories. Speaking of which, I have to get back. I'm determined to get more information on these mysteries."

Mary fell silent as they walked back. She knew she'd lost him, that she was no longer the center of his attention. But at least it wasn't to another woman. It was to his writing. She wondered, idly, if some day she'd see his name on a book cover.

Cynthia Fitch called Bert Ward's room. "Come over now. He's gone for a while. I need to talk with you."

Moments later, at his knock, she opened the door to him, glanced up and down the corridor while he stepped inside, then closed the door. He took a chair and she stood in front of him.

She glared. "You're the private detective, and I have to do your work. David's been seeing that woman. Patricia August."

Ward avoided her eyes. "I haven't caught him at it."

"You've been too busy downing beer and ale downstairs." She paced up and down in front of him. "You've had a free hand, here. No one knew your true role, and they still don't. Well, I've seen him go to her. Twice. That's two times more than you have. But you have the camera. And I need photos—not just your eyewitness testimony, which I don't have yet, either. I need incriminating photographs. So far, you've given me nothing."

He squirmed. "We're still here. I'll get some shots."

"Look, Ward, I've paid you well these two months. But the only thing you've done right is conceal your mission from David. I'll give you that—at least David doesn't suspect anything."

His lips turned up. "So I play a good part as a flunky, somebody to carry suitcases."

She sniffed. "Maybe that's your highest and best calling." Her eyes narrowed, watching him. "So what will you do now?"

Ward took a deep breath. "I'll get on his tail from now on. I'll get some photographs. You can count on it."

She saw that's all she could expect. "Then I'll give you some help. Here's my plan. Tonight, at ten, I'll tell David I have a headache, and I'm going to bed, taking sleeping powders. I know where he'll head right after that—to her room. Follow him. And don't fail this time. Catch them together."

Ward nodded. "I'll catch them. And I'll get photos."

In Armand's Restaurant, John and Penny Darnell took seats at their regular window table, which the head waiter took them to automatically when they entered. "It's your table," Bardon had told Darnell, "whenever you want it."

Darnell gazed out at the rainswept street and the clouds above. "The weather matches the mood in this hotel."

"When will this end, John?"

"At least we have no ghost anymore. Since I challenged Adrian on that . . ."

Ernest Hemingway approached the table, limping along with his cane. When he reached it, he said, "Professor? May I talk with you?"

Darnell glanced quickly at Penny, who nodded,

and said, "Of course. Take a seat there." He watched as Hemingway eased himself into the chair.

"Your legs must bother you a lot," Penny said.

He smiled. "A canister filled with many metal fragments exploded near me. I got it in the legs. Over two hundred separate flesh wounds, and over two hundred scars. Some of it is too deep for them to remove it. It's still there." He glanced from Darnell to Penny. "Oh, I'm sorry. Maybe I shouldn't have gone into that."

Darnell shook his head. "Not at all. We hope your legs continue to improve."

"They will." He looked at Darnell. "The thing is, sir, if I might—I was a reporter before the war. *Kansas City Star*, in America. I want to write. In fact, I've been taking notes here, during all this, to get an article going. I'll be returning to the states in a little over a week, and I'd like to make it a good story."

Darnell said, "I think I hear a request coming."

"Well, it's just this—if you could share with me any insights you have, any information that isn't too private, that would help me a lot. If I could just be around more when things are happening, like a reporter might be, I could do a better story."

Darnell nodded. "I understand. And from what you said, you realize some of what happens is police business and can't be revealed in an ongoing case. But I'll see what we can do. I'll talk with the Inspector. If you're around—I know you have other things you're interested in—we'll see about involving you in some way."

"That's all I could ask. I'll stay close at hand. I might be underfoot, as we say." He rose, with some difficulty, leaning on the cane. "Thank you, Professor. And Mrs. Darnell."

Darnell shook his hand, and Hemingway hobbled away.

The waiter approached and took their simple orders, soup and sandwiches and coffee.

"An ambitious young man," Penny said. "And brave."

"Yes. It took some courage just to ask me for help."

"And I'm sure you'll give him some."

"Within limits. Inspector Manot is in charge of the case."

"So—what else are you doing?"

"Manot is obtaining search warrants. We'll be looking for evidence. He has one or two lines of inquiry, and I have some of my own." He grimaced. "But I'm getting this feeling, Penny—you know how it is with me at this stage of a case."

"You start seeing things in your mind, things you think could happen. Predicting. Worrying."

"I'm not psychic—I don't even believe in that sort of thing; you know that. But I'll be surprised if something else disastrous doesn't happen in the next twenty-four hours. I've just always been able to sense that kind of danger."

She smiled. "Feel it in your bones?"

"In my gut, maybe."

"Then maybe you're just hungry." Her eyes twinkled. "Let's see how you feel after lunch." She looked up as the waiter brought their soup and served it, and they ate silently for some moments.

She eyed him over the top of her teacup. "You haven't told me much about the case lately. It might be important for me to know, John. I'm in the middle of this, too."

Darnell sat back. "You're right. But everything we have is marginal and not proven in any way." He paused to sip his coffee. "Now remember—anything I say is for you only, not for any others who are here—your lunch companions, the women."

"John, please. I should know all that by now. How long have I been married to a detective? Six years?"

"All right." Darnell told her about the talking script and how it might be important as motivation. "Manot's convinced both murders were made to get the script. And it is missing, and we do have to find it." He patted the pocket containing Eric Thorndyke's notebook. "I still have to read Eric Thorndyke's notebook in detail."

The waiter brought the sandwiches and coffee. They began eating.

Penny spoke between bites. "There's a lot of uncertainty."

"It's too early to decide too much. I'm reserving judgment. One thing I am certain of is that we're dealing with a clever, devious, and dangerous adversary. If we jump to conclusions too soon, we may never solve this."

Penny nodded. "But you've got that unknown factor—your instinct warning you something could happen today. Or tonight."

Throughout the afternoon, while Penny sought out Sylvia Beach and strolled among the mezzanine shops, Darnell circulated about the hotel observing the players in the still-unfolding drama, wherever they were evident. The soldier, who caught up with him in the lobby, walked about with him, talking. Darnell chose his words carefully, so as not to reveal Manot's plans.

Philip Thorndyke seemed to have taken to his room again. Ward could be seen nowhere. Darnell walked through the brasserie casually with Hemingway, as if chatting, and noticed the Spaniard sat in a booth with a tall bottle of red wine, half full, on the table in front of him. And as they left the room, Darnell saw Edda Van Eych heading toward the booth.

Having seen what little he could, and anxious to hear from Manot, Darnell parted with Hemingway at the hotel exit and took a long, bracing walk on the boulevard. On his return he went to their room and settled in for a thorough reading of Eric Thorndyke's notebook. As he read descriptions of scenes for the proposed film, he saw in his mind's eye the young, blond woman with a sweater around her shoulders, tears in her eyes, waving at the distinguised man as he walked away, her posture showing it was a sad good-bye. Darnell was shocked to learn that the script contemplated the young woman being married already to a much older, very wealthy man. He recalled the earlier reference to the eternal love triangle. This was it.

When Penny returned, they decided to have food sent up to the room, and spent the evening together there. The phone call came in at eight p.m. that night.

"Louis," Darnell said, "what news do you have?"

"I could not get the search warrants issued today. Each one is individual. Tomorrow morning I will reach judges. I expect to knock on your door not long after noon."

"Call first."

"*Oui* . . . anything happening there?"

"Like a morgue."

Darnell could almost see Manot grimace when he said, *"Mon Dieu!* That is exactly what Chief Inspector Guerin said to me this morning. Only he called the hotel my own private morgue."

Chapter Eighteen

Sunday night, December 29

Bert Ward looked up and down the ninth-floor corridor of Le Grand Hotel at nine-thirty that night, making sure it was deserted before he began his activities. His box camera strung around his neck by a leather strap, other equipment in his left hand, he crossed to the door of the Martin Prince suite. With the practiced skill of years of entering forbidden places, he quickly opened the side bedroom door of the suite with a lock pick, and softly closed the door behind him after being certain no one had come into the hallway or seen him enter the room.

Turning on no lights, Ward worked his way across the rooms slowly in the ambient light from the street. The moon was visible in the now-clear sky, the Eiffel Tower a striking profile in the distance. Knowing it might be partly imagination, Ward felt he breathed the smell of death. Martin Prince's death.

Passing the connecting door between Prince's room and Patricia August's, he stopped and listened. No sound. He pictured her sitting, anxiously waiting on the other side of the door, just as he would wait, until Fitch's predictable arrival.

The sound of Fitch entering her room came just

after ten o'clock, David Fitch obviously wasting no time. Holding an ear close to the door, Ward could make out Fitch's familiar voice, and then the gentler sounds of the woman. He heard the words, "Trisha," and "David," among the other hushed rumblings of their voices. Then the sounds became softer and more distant, and Ward suspected they moved toward the bedroom by the balcony—his own ultimate destination.

He crossed to Prince's balcony and opened the door, as silent as he could be, given the his size and usual clumsy style of movement that his London partner once called rhinoceroslike. Outside, he glanced across to the balcony jutting out from Patricia August's rooms, and saw faint light emanating from the windows. The draperies were open. They expected no intrusion of their privacy on the ninth floor of a hotel at this hour, with no other buildings opposite or in near-enough view. As in his case, they could move about in the street's light, with little other illumination.

He waited for a few moments, allowing them to settle themselves into the room. Not at all naive, given his profession, he knew what he was about to see in the room could be extremely embarrassing to the occupants, exactly what Cynthia Fitch wanted. His testimony would be important, as any denial on their part could be proved to be perjury in a courtroom. And in any case, what he would tell Cynthia Fitch would give her a wedge for what she wanted to accomplish. The problem was taking the photograph, but she insisted, and he had to try. The flash equipment was awkward and cumbersome, and he anticipated problems.

Allowing a little more time, he went to the railing

and sized up the distance to the other balcony. More than two feet, almost three. He could step over to the next railing, using care, grasping the rail with one hand, holding the camera equipment with the other. He stepped over the rail to stand on the six-inch ledge protruding below the rail. He reached across, gripped the rail of the other balcony, and placed one foot on its ledge. He balanced himself on both ledges, one foot now on each. No problem so far, he thought, standing astride the space between the ledges of the two balconies. But he looked down, a mistake because of the height, and quickly raised his eyes back up to his level, took a deep breath, and steadied himself.

He stepped across with his other foot, and put a leg over the railing. In a moment, he stood fully on the other balcony, breathing hard. He was not within view of the windows, not visible to anyone who might be looking out. He prepared his camera flash equipment, an eight-inch-long metal trough, two inches wide and a half-inch deep, attached to a long pole. He took a bag from his pocket and poured the contents, a mixture of magnesium, phosphorous, and other powders, into the trough.

He lit a cigarette and obliquely peered through a window. Patricia August, nude, stood in the embrace of David Fitch, who also wore no clothing. When Fitch enveloped her again in his arms, Ward held the flash trough in his left hand above his head, touched his cigarette to the powder, tossed his cigarette away, brought his camera to his eye, and sighted. The exploding flash powder made a sharp noise and created a bright light for several seconds, long enough for him to click the shutter on the front of the camera and snap the picture. He dropped the trough, know-

ing the bright light startled them. It also had un-
nerved him, in the dark night. His figure silhouetted
against the outside light, and he hoped they would
not recognize him, but he had to move fast. He
whirled back to the railing, his camera dangling by
the strap held in one hand. *I must not lose the camera!*

He stepped over the railing, reaching out again
with one hand and one foot across to Prince's balcony ledge, but, in his haste, his foot slipped off.
Trying again, he realized the camera strap was slid-
ing from the grasp of his sweaty hand, and he heard
the door behind him opening. Now trying to hold
the camera, step over the rail, and gain a foothold
on the other ledge, he reached across with his foot
but lost his balance.

His heart raced, and his mouth was dry. Behind him,
he heard the noise of the door to the balcony opening,
and footsteps. He could not look back, as he released
his handgrip on the railing momentarily to secure the
camera, to grip it more firmly. But it fell away from
his grasp, tumbling down toward the ground, end over
end, and at the same moment Ward lost his one good
foothold on Trisha August's ledge.

He reached out for the railing too late, and realized
to his horror he couldn't quite grasp it, and he had
no foothold or handhold on either balcony. It was as
if he were suddenly pushed away from his only secure hold. Ward plunged down between the two balconies toward the ground, unbelieving of his fate,
screaming for all nine floors in a gurgling, high-
pitched voice no one, least of all himself, could identify as his own, uttering the last, horrible sounds of
his life.

*   *   *

Darnell heard the scream as he lay in bed next to a sleeping Penny. When he rushed out on the balcony, she stirred also, rose, and peered through the window. Darnell saw the body there, not identifiable, smashed and bloody, arms and legs at bizarre angles. A small crowd already was forming a semicircle around it, and three policemen elbowed their way into its midst.

Darnell threw on shirt, pants, and shoes and ran to the elevator carrying his jacket. In the lobby, as he passed by the front desk, he told the agitated head desk clerk, René Alain, to call the doctor, Bardon, and Inspector Manot. He pulled on his jacket while running to the street toward the officers. He looked at the body, asked the officers, "Do you speak English?"

When one nodded, Darnell said, "I know this man. I've been working with your Inspector Manot, and I've asked the hotel clerk to call him out here. Keep the crowd back. Keep them away."

The officer nodded, evidently understanding English well enough. He spoke harshly in French to the growing crowd of passersby, who stepped back a few feet as he motioned to them to keep their distance. Then the officers turned and joined the other dozen sets of eyes that stared with disbelief and morbid fascination at the broken body of Bert Ward.

Hemingway arrived, limping down the sidewalk toward the crowd, wearing civilian clothing and shoes instead of his heavy cordovan boots. He came up next to Darnell, breathing hard, looked at the body, and exchanged a glance with Darnell.

Bardon arrived next, followed in moments by Dr. Pascal, who stepped forward to the body and examined it. Manot's car pulled up at the curb as the doctor finished his examination and stood, turning to face Manot. He shook his head and stepped aside.

"*Mon Dieu!*" Manot looked at Darnell with wide eyes, then approached the body gingerly, avoiding the splatters of blood, with Darnell stepping forward alongside. "What happened, John?"

"I heard the man scream and looked down. I couldn't recognize him from the height, but ran down, asked the clerk to make some calls, and came out. Then I saw it was Bert Ward."

Inspector Manot glanced at the two *gendarmes*, and asked them a question in French. When they shook their heads, he turned back to the body. "They did not see him fall, John."

Darnell stared up at the hotel. "There are two balconies almost above the body. He may have fallen from one of them."

"But what was he doing up there?"

Darnell said, "We'd best talk inside."

Manot nodded. "Yes, of course. I'll leave two men in charge." He gave brief orders to them in French, then turned to the hotel manager and doctor. "M'sieur Bardon and Dr. Pascal, please come with us." He marched into the hotel with Darnell, Bardon, an officer, and the doctor in step with him, passed a wide-eyed René Alain to a small glassed-in office behind the front desk. Ernest Hemingway followed some distance back.

"Quickly, now," Manot said. "Dr. Pascal, did you see anything, ah, unusual—any special marks on the body to explain this?"

"No. It seems to be a fall only. But—well, naturally it is hard to tell with the body in that condition."

Darnell said, "You're thinking he may have struggled with someone who overpowered him, struck him, and threw him down?"

Manot's smile was grim. "The policeman must always think of those possibilities."

Bardon said in a disconsolate voice, "A third death in my hotel . . . I'll have to call the Chairman immmediately."

"I need someone to stay with the body, Doctor, until the medical examiner arrives," Manot said. "Will you do that?"

Dr. Pascal nodded.

Manot motioned to Darnell. "Up to the ninth floor. We'll look into the rooms in that area."

As they ran to the elevator, Darnell said, "As I recall the layout, the two rooms closest to the position of his body are Patricia August's and Martin Prince's suite."

Manot grimaced. "Is it Martin Prince's ghost now, John? Knocking guests in the head? Throwing them over the railing?"

Hemingway missed the elevator they took but waited impatiently for the next one. In minutes, he, too, was walking down the corridor toward Martin Prince's suite.

David Fitch stepped back inside, closed the balcony door, and threw on clothes while Trisha August pulled on a nightgown. He opened the door to the hall, watching as Professor Darnell ran from his room to the elevator. Hearing the elevator door close and the car begin its descent, he ran back to his room with key in hand. Entering, he closed the door gently, not to wake Cynthia, although if she had taken sleeping powders she would be oblivious even to the man's horrible screams.

But others on the floor would have heard it, and would soon be dressing and going down to the scene. He realized what he must do, what any normally curious person would do—go down to the street. He straightened his clothing and grabbed a jacket.

Cynthia's voice called. "David? What's happening?"

He walked to the bedroom and looked in at her. She stood in her nightgown at the closed window, looking out but turning toward him as he entered. Her startled eyes were filled with questioning and fear, much more than with mere curiosity.

"I don't know. Someone may have fallen." He went to the balcony door, opened it, and stepped out, looking down. "My God," he said. "It's true. A man's body . . ."

She came out beside him and stared down. She said nothing.

He turned to her. "You didn't take your powders?"

"N-no. Where were you?"

"I needed something from a shop. I heard the man scream as I was coming back."

"Then you knew it was a man?"

He motioned below. "Well, it's clear—"

"You're lying, David." Her eyes flashed. She whirled and stepped back inside.

He followed. "Do you want to explain yourself?"

"You were with that woman. Patricia August."

David stopped in midstride. He felt his mouth drop open, then clenched his teeth tightly. *Damn!*

She knows about her! He could not answer. He walked into the bathroom and closed the door to get his bearings.

"Coward!" He heard her voice outside the door, and she pounded on it several times, then burst into tears.

Fitch splashed water onto his face and smoothed his hair back. Incredible! Someone was spying on them and fell to his death while doing it. Cynthia knew about him and Trisha. Then he realized *she* had sent the intruder. *She* was behind it all. Trying to prove he and Trisha . . . He took a deep breath. Nothing to do now but face the situation.

John Darnell listened as Inspector Manot questioned Patricia August. She wore a chenille robe and slippers and sat on the sofa. Hemingway kept well back near the door, listening.

"You say the scream woke you?"

"Yes. I'd retired early. I was almost asleep, drifting off, but when I heard it I sat up and knew it was real, somehow. I went to the window and looked out, but I didn't look at the ground right away. In a few minutes I heard other noises, like a crowd, looked down, and saw the body."

Manot frowned. "Mademoiselle, it appears he fell either from your balcony or the next one—Martin Prince's suite. You knew nothing of that?"

She shook her head.

"We may inspect your balcony?"

"Of course."

Manot strode to the balcony door and opened it. Darnell followed him outside. They peered down at the body that Darnell could see lay on the ground almost directly below either this balcony or the next one.

Manot said, "The other suite, M'sieur Prince's, is now unoccupied. It is locked. This one seems more likely."

Darnell nodded. He walked back and forth on the balcony slowly, then stopped suddenly and stooped down. He touched a powdery substance on the balcony floor. "What do you make of this, Louis?"

Manot stooped over and rubbed his fingers back and forth in the small quantity of powder. He took an envelope from his pocket and scooped into it as much of the powder as he could find, sealed, and pocketed it. "I will have it analyzed, but I think it is photographic powder."

"I agree." Darnell looked back through the window at the woman, still seated in her chair, not looking their way. "She is acting a good part."

"Something violent happened out here," Manot said.

"Indeed. Ward attempted to take a photograph. But why?" He leaned over and looked closely at the Prince balcony and the dark room, and gestured. "That door is ajar. That was Ward's escape route, stepping over from this balcony to the next one. Somehow he fell, or was pushed." He nodded. "Louis, you have much to talk about with Miss August."

Manot nodded. He called Patricia August into the room and held up the small packet of powder to show what they had found on the balcony. "A photograph was being taken from your balcony. We believe someone was here with you. A man. Who was it?"

Patricia broke down in tears. In a moment, she composed herself and said, "David Fitch." She rose, went to her closet and produced the photographic trough. "I cleaned up the powder residue from the balcony."

Manot summoned Fitch into the room and confronted him.

Fitch fumed. "Damned meddler, Ward! Yes, we were together," he said defiantly, "but it was personal and private. He had no damned business . . ."

"So, m'sieur—you ran out on the balcony, struggled with him, and threw him over the edge."

"No—no! He fell off."

Manot looked at Trisha August.

"That's true," she said.

Fitch scowled. "My own man—I just don't know what to make of it. Some scheme for money, perhaps. Sell some photographs to a sensationalist journal, or blackmail—to sell them back to me."

Manot left the two people together after saying he would need written statements the next day. He and Darnell returned to the sidewalk scene below and located the smashed camera.

"So it appears Ward had a little sideline," Darnell said. "Perhaps he took the job with them strictly for that reason."

"We will examine the film."

"If you're lucky, and if the film is intact, you may see one very revealing photograph."

Manot said, "Proving nothing. Do you think Fitch and Ward fought?"

"Fitch and Patricia August are the only witnesses."

He shook his head. "There's no way to know, unless you find something on Ward's body to incriminate Fitch." Darnell smiled. "Like a button conveniently torn from Fitch's garment."

Manot's smile was grim. "I suspect Fitch wore no garment."

John Darnell knew Penny would want to know everything, and when he found her waiting for him in their room with some impatience, he plunged into the story, including the explanation of Ward's spying on Fitch and Patricia, the photographing, and his fall.

"The only witnesses could be lying," he said. "We have no way of knowing. But with the timing and circumstances, it appears unlikely Fitch fought with Ward on the balcony. Ward probably fell before Fitch could even get out there in his obvious state of, shall we say, undress."

"Poor Ward. A horrible way to die. That scream— I heard it in my dreams. It's going to be hard to forget."

Darnell said, "Manot and I have a busy day ahead tomorrow. Cynthia Fitch."

"That should be interesting. . . . John, I remember what you said yesterday—that you felt something would happen in the next twenty-four hours. Well it has. When will it all end?"

"Ward's death was accidental, but in the larger scheme, it must have something to do with the two murders." He frowned. "We'll see if we can find the connection tomorrow."

When he sat next to her on the bed, she put an arm around him and said, "I'll be glad when we get back to London, John, so we can talk like human beings, like a family, about more important things than ghosts and murder." But when he turned to look at her quizzically, she added, "No—I don't mean that. I'm not going alone. Don't think that for a minute! Just get this case over with."

Chapter Nineteen

Monday morning, December 30

The day broke with bright sun streaming through the windows of the Darnells' rooms, but it was the phone ringing that woke Darnell. He glanced at a clock—eight a.m. When he picked up the phone, Manot's now-familiar voice came over the instrument.

"We have, what you call, John, unfinished business."

"Cynthia Fitch?"

"Yes. The search warrants—they will be here about twelve, but we should speak with Mrs. Fitch earlier."

"At nine a.m., then? Meet me in the lobby for coffee?"

Manot agreed, and Darnell showered, dressed, and said a hasty good-bye to Penny. "I'll see you at lunchtime," he said.

In the lobby a few minutes early, he stepped outside for a breath of Paris air and to watch for Manot. He examined the area where Ward's body had lain and saw bloodstains not yet cleaned.

Instinctively, he looked up toward the two balconies involved in the drama of the night before and saw Trisha August standing on hers, alone. He could only imagine her thoughts this morning, as well as those plaguing David and Cynthia Fitch. The scandal was out in the open. The three of them would have to struggle with it, each differently, and the police and he would have to read between the lines.

Manot's car drove up, and he jumped out. The driver continued on.

Darnell pointed to the café just inside the door. "Coffee?"

"Definitely. We need to talk."

They settled at a table, and a waiter brought coffee. After downing his first small cup quickly, Manot motioned for more.

"We will have the warrants at two p.m.," Manot said. "Then we can commence our search for that script."

"Any of them would have had time to conceal it elsewhere. But, on the other hand, whoever has it may not realize we suspect its importance. It could still be in the hotel."

"And you suggest?"

"Tonight at, say, seven or eight o'clock, you gather everyone in the Prince group together in room 999. Tell them it is to reexamine what happened at that original party on the seventeenth. You can position the guests in their spots as they were just before the death of Eric Thorndyke. Ask them what they saw and heard at that time. It may bring back recollections."

"Interrogate them again?"

"Yes."

"You would not be there?"

"I'll accompany your officers with the warrants, and search every room while all the occupants are occupied, held there by you. We'd have the element of surprise."

"We won't have the warrrants until two. We could wait a few hours. Yes, I will clear it with Chief Inspector Guerin. So—now, Madame Fitch. She knows we are coming. We need her side of this sordid story."

David Fitch glared at his wife with ill-disguised hatred. "I see everything now. It was you who urged me to hire Ward. Said your friend recommended him, said he could take care of suitcases and reservations. All bloody lies. You wanted him around to spy on me, and to take photographs. You think I don't know why?"

"Why?" Her eyes blazed. "Because I don't like my husband sleeping with another woman."

Fitch laughed, realizing there was a touch of hysteria in his voice. "Well, you'd better get used to it. I'm getting a divorce. And, more's the point, you'll be back on the street, where you belong."

The knock on the door caught their attention. Fitch looked at Cynthia, straightened his tie. "Your *Sûreté* friend," he said.

She brushed tears from her eyes and went to the door. She admitted Manot and Darnell and led the way to a sitting area. "You wanted to talk," she managed to say, looking at Manot.

Fitch could see she was avoiding his eyes. Good reason, he thought—yet, in his back of his mind, something nagged. A conscience? A memory of how it was with her those first years?

Manot cleared his throat. "We know certain things, madame. Mr. Ward was your employee. We found papers on his body showing he was a private detective." He turned to Fitch. "Ward lost his life after taking photos of you, M'sieur Fitch, with Mademoiselle August."

Fitch shook his head. "A detective!"

Manot said, "He had a thousand English pounds in his wallet."

Cynthia's eyebrows went up, and she stared at Manot.

"You sent Bert Ward there, Mrs. Fitch? You instructed him to take photographs?"

"He was my husband, with a—a common whore . . ."

"Bloody hell!" Fitch stood and strode to the window and looked out. He could feel his rage bubbling up again. "I don't have to listen to this."

"Do you feel responsible for his death, madame?"

"Of course not. Ask David about responsibility. He was there. Maybe he pushed him off the balcony."

Fitch whirled around and walked back in front of his wife and stared at her, clenching and unclenching his fists. Somehow, he found control, saying to himself, *Watch it, David!*—words he always said to himself when he was about to make a serious mistake. *No violence!*

"Go ahead, hit me," she said.

Fitch turned away and threw himself on the sofa.

Darnell turned to Inspector Manot. "What can you say about the camera? The film?"

Manot nodded. "The fall of the camera was stopped near the ground by some bushes. It was damaged, but the film may be saved."

Cynthia Fitch looked up sharply from her study of the carpet at her feet. "That would be my film, Inspector."

"It is evidence, madame."

"But I bought that camera, the film, equipment . . ."

Fitch made an unintelligible sound and gripped the arm of the sofa.

"We accomplish nothing more, here." Manot stood, scowling. "I will send my assistant to obtain your written statements."

Out in the corridor, Manot said to Darnell, "Ward had a thousand pounds in his wallet. Payment for some devious scheme. Those two people, each in their own way for their own greedy reasons, caused a man's death. And I can do nothing about it. Unless we can prove Fitch fought with him, it stays an accident."

Manot headed back to his office, saying to Darnell that he was going "to fume, to sulk, to bleed awhile."

Darnell nodded. "When you finish bleeding, and have the warrants in your pockets, and Chief Inspector Guerin blesses the idea of the gathering tonight—call me. I'll be ready for a long night."

John and Penny Darnell took their regular table in Armand's restaurant. The crisp, clear air of Paris afforded them an inspiring view of the city, and they lingered after lunch, talking, with no critical activity needed until the evening.

"John, tomorrow's the last day of this year," Penny said.

"Yes. And I know it's a time for celebration."

"Will you solve this case in time to celebrate?"

"The case will solve itself soon. Something will tell us it's over."

"Something connected with Thorndyke's ghost, or that movie script?"

"Perhaps both."

With time to spare, Darnell suggested they take a

long walk. "I haven't been out of this hotel more than a few hours in four days."

They strolled down the Champs-Elysses Boulevard to the Arc de Triomphe, stopped in several shops, took another cup of coffee in a sidewalk café, and worked their way back to the hotel about sunset. Taking the elevator up to their floor, Darnell was fidgety. As they entered their room, the phone rang and Darnell scooped it up as Penny went on into their bedroom.

The Inspector's voice sounded eager. "It is Manot. I tried to reach you several times. I'm on my way out."

"Good. I'm anxious to get started. Come to my room."

Inspector Manot reached Darnell's door just before six p.m. and upon entering spread the folders he carried on a table. "The warrants," he said. "One for each room of all the parties."

"And the gathering tonight? What have you done?"

"Calls were made from headquarters. They've all been notified to come to room 999 at exactly eight p.m."

"Let's review the list."

Manot nodded, and flipped over each slender folder as he talked. "Patricia August, now the representative of American-Universal, replacing Martin Prince. David and Cynthia Fitch. Edda Van Eych, the Dutch writer. Ricardo Camilo, the Spanish writer."

"I see you pair those two together."

"Précisément. Brandon Tyler, the English publisher. Philip Thorndyke, of course, to host the affair. Sylvia

Beach. The young actress from America, Mary Miles Minter, and her mother, Charlotte Shelby. Those are all the names. Down to ten, now."

"The soldier, Ernest Hemingway, is a reporter, at least he will be when he returns to America."

"He was not at that first party. We don't need him there."

"Right. He wants to observe the proceedings, to write his story."

"We can't tell him about the search."

"I know. But he might prove useful sometime tonight. His friend, the actress, will be at the party. He'll have time."

"You can keep him available, but he can't know our plans."

"Of course."

Manot said, "I brought four *policier*—uniformed officers. Two for your assistance in the searches, and two to be stationed in Prince's suite and to escort any of the guests there if needed. Bardon, as hotel *Directeur*, will join the search, and he will come here to your room before eight with my officers."

"We have some time to spare."

"And I have a table for three reserved for a quick dinner at Armand's. We can return by seven-thirty."

In minutes, John and Penny Darnell joined Inspector Manot as he strode purposefully toward the elevators.

Philip Thorndyke did not look forward to the events of the evening. The Inspector made it all sound very routine, very cozy, having all the guests in Prince's suite for a replay. But thinking of the horrible event of that Tuesday night, one day short of two weeks earlier, and thinking of what happened behind that bedroom door, he felt a combination of anger and regret. The ice-cold champagne he poured for himself helped, numbing his feelings.

But the image of his father lying in the death chair would not leave his mind. Could he have done anything to keep the night's events from ending in that horrific way? The Inspector would no doubt explore the same question as to all the guests.

Seven o'clock now, and as he sat sipping champagne on the sofa he could hear caterers rattling the tables and bottles into Prince's suite. They'd be setting up the hors d'oeuvres, wine and champagne glasses, champagne bottles in ice buckets along the tables along with several bottles of red wine. Everything as close as possible to the way the room was set up the night his father was murdered. But Manot's ultimate goal of the evening eluded him. The police had something up their sleeves, and he wished he knew what that was.

The knock at his door brought him out of his thoughts, and he stepped over to the door, glass still in hand. He opened it to Adrian.

"Well, the magician. Here to do some magic tricks?"

In a low voice, Adrian said, "Maybe pull some money out of a hat. I'll take the money you promised me and save you a trip tonight. You've had plenty of time to go to your bank." Adrian brushed past him. "I noticed preparations for a party out there."

"A party of sorts, old chap, of sorts." Thorndyke gulped the rest of his champagne, and scowled. "I don't have your damned money here. It's in my deposit box at the front desk. You'll get it, after the party, after your last show, as we agreed.''

Adrian glared at Thorndyke, said nothing, stalked to the door, and walked out into the hall toward the stairs.

Chapter Twenty

Monday night, December 30

At seven-thirty p.m., John and Penny Darnell and Inspector Manot entered the Darnells' room, just as the phone rang. "Take it, Louis," Darnell said.

Manot answered the phone, nodding, saying, "Excellent." He told Darnell, "My men will be up here soon. They all speak English well. And the party begins at eight. The wine and hors d'oeuvres will keep them there long enough for you to complete your searches, and, if not, my men will."

"When we finish, we'll let you know at once. At some point someone there may begin to suspect something."

At a knock on the door, Manot admitted four uniformed *Sûreté* officers, and directed them to chairs. He explained the search procedures again, and the assignment of each. The two assigned to Darnell nodded at him as Manot continued his talk.

Manot handed the search warrants to the senior officer of the two. "These are your authority to enter each room, the number shown. Search thoroughly. Professor Darnell will guide you as to what types of things to look for, what might be unusual, and will evaluate what you find. Show him anything questionable."

Penny stepped out of the bedroom into the living room and over to Darnell. "Do I look presentable for the party?"

He admired her dress and smiled. "I wish I were going with you."

"It's almost eight o'clock," she said, looking at Manot.

A knock came at the door. Manot said, "It's the *Directeur*."

By eight-fifteen, Prince's suite buzzed with conversation, noise of glasses clinking, sounds of silverware against china—just as if it were a true party. But Philip Thorndyke thought a sense of false gaiety permeated the atmosphere. This, he told himself, could be one very interesting, excruciating evening. He recalled the night of the first party with a sense of déjà vu, and also a sense of impending doom, probably brought on by the repetition of events.

He watched as Inspector Manot moved about the room, talking to people one by one or in groups about their positions in the room, confirming where they were standing at times before the body of Eric Thorndyke was discovered, and it seemed to him that Manot relished the sense of anticipation and uncertainty that all felt. Nothing seeming private, and given his own personal stake in the proceedings—a discovery perhaps of vital information regarding his father's death—Philip felt justified in tagging along near Manot and listening in on the early conversations. Manot did not object. But as Philip walked about, observing, it was increasingly through the prism of the glow of the champagne, as symbolized by the glass, ever present in his hand.

Having positioned everyone, Manot said he would soon start his interrogations. To Philip, at hand, he said, "I will come back to you last, to talk about your finding your father's body. I'll begin now with Cynthia Fitch."

Inspector Manot surveyed the room. Cynthia Fitch stood at the other side of the grand piano, at the edge of the room most distant from the bedroom where Eric Thorndyke died. As he walked toward her, he noticed Philip Thorndyke again following him. He turned to him. "No, m'sieur. From now on, I must do this alone." He waited until Thorndyke, obviously disappointed, had turned and gone back to the position Manot had selected for him. But even as Manot began his work, he realized it was mostly a charade, and part of his mind was out there on the ninth floor with his men and Darnell and the search. He didn't like this process, although others might think he did, but it seemed the only way to maintain surprise. He took a deep breath and approached Mrs. Cynthia Fitch.

"I understand, madame," Manot said, "you had a strong conversation that evening with Mr. Eric Thorndyke." He gestured about the area, glanced up at the chandelier overhead. "Just about here, others have said."

Her lip curled into a harsh smile. "Others, yes—others with big ears." She glared sharply across a short space to the other side of the piano where Edda Van Eych stood, holding a glass of champagne, in the position she told Manot she had held at that juncture that night.

"And you were discussing—in that manner?"

"We've gone over all this before."

"Not in these surroundings, not in such a way that others can observe, others whom we can also ask what happened."

Her gaze was cold. "You want to catch one of us in a lie?"

"Madame, I ask the questions. Once more, what did you talk about that raised your voices—and tempers?"

She breathed in slowly. "My husband and Mr. Thorndyke had been having some business talks for some time, not only here but previously, in London. Investments, film projects, I don't know. Thorndyke was drinking heavily that night and got very personal. He told me my husband was having an affair."

"He told you it was Patricia August?"

"Yes. I had suspected someone. That's why I had employed Ward. But until we came here, I wasn't sure who it was."

"What did you tell Thorndyke?"

"I said I didn't believe him. But of course I knew it was true. That's what made me so angry. That even a relative stranger like Thorndyke knew about it."

"He spoke of his project?"

She shook her head. "Only vaguely. A Hollywood deal of some sort."

"Relax, madame. Take that chair. That's all I need for now."

He stepped over to Mary Miles Minter, some feet away, standing alone. Nearby stood Patricia August and within a few feet in another direction, Charlotte Shelby. Manot asked the young girl, "You were standing about here for some time with Mr. Fitch, *n'est-ce pas?*"

When he was about to apologize for his French,

she said, "I understand you, Inspector. I'm fluent in your language."

Manot inclined his head. "Then you also understand why I ask the questions?"

"Of course. A man dies. A second man dies. A third man dies. You ask questions. You're a policeman, right?"

"Standing here, recalling the night, is there anything you can tell me about Mr. Fitch's attitude. Was he agitated? Did he confide in you? Perhaps here you remember better."

"All I remember is how he kept touching my arms. It was embarrassing. My mother was over there, as she is." She pointed at her. "And Mr. Prince's associate, Miss August, just there."

"But when I talked with you and your mother, she said it was Mr. Eric Thorndyke who was, ah, annoying you."

"Yes, he did. They both did. All men do. But as to Mr. Fitch, well, my mother knew he was very wealthy and she wanted to see what he could do for us—for *me*, she would say. So she didn't complain about him as much. Didn't want to disturb any dealings. Money is very important to my mother."

"Back to Eric Thorndyke. Did he talk with you about his project?"

Mary looked around the room, caught the eye of her mother on her. "He told me about the script. I told my mother later. I never saw it, of course."

"He seemed to say it was ideal for you."

"Yes. But I don't know much more than that. My mother became obsessed with it, the more she heard."

"Yes. And I thank you. Now just enjoy the evening."

He turned and walked the few steps to Patricia August, realizing now why the woman would have been disturbed, seeing Fitch's attentions to the young girl, whom she could have seen as a rival. A mantel clock showed Manot the time to be eight-thirty. He was gaining some insights into previous behavior of the suspects, and in his mind they were all still suspects. But more importantly, he knew his men must be deep into the searches by now. With no one in the hotel rooms it should proceed fast.

Officers had searched the room of Bert Ward first, before the party, without any success, as well as the room Sylvia Beach stayed in, and her apartment. Now, Darnell and the officers inspected the Thorndykes' suite, and Brandon Tyler's room, finding only the usual clothing and travel gear.

"Next, Professor?" Jacques Bardon asked.

"Five rooms to go. Let's take the room of the actress and her mother now." That search, as in the others, involved going through closets, dressers, cupboards, suitcases, and under and behind furniture, and yielded nothing pertinent. Darnell was struck by the photos of the actress and a much older, distinguished gentleman, found tucked away in the young actress's suitcase. He disliked the personal aspects of this kind of inquiry, but saw no alternative.

"Camilo," he announced next. "Remember, any device resembling a garotte. A long thin cord or strip of leather. He's the most likely one to have something like that." But no such device was found.

In Patricia August's room, the officers pointed out the residual powder spills from the flash trough she had concealed there, but that added nothing to what they already knew. He reminded the officers to leave all articles in the same condition in which they found them.

"The Fitches' room, now," he said. The search also produced nothing of note, except that he shook his head, surprised, when the officers pointed out bundles of English pounds and French francs merely lying loose in drawers.

"The last room is that of Edda Van Eych. Maybe she conceals something," he said to Bardon. When the search ended Darnell frowned as he told Bardon, "All she conceded was that she was German, not Dutch. She probably felt it was safer to be Dutch in Paris in 1918."

Manot probed the feelings of the guests who held their positions until interviewed and then mingled with the others, but none being allowed to leave suite 999. Manot had continued on with his interrogations, learning little although generally accomplishing what he and Darnell really wanted—for his men to complete the searches.

He learned little from Brandon Tyler, except his concern about a continuation of his contract. "I hope," Tyler said, "new policies may help in that."

"So Mr. Prince's death works to your advantage?"

Tyler hastily said, "I just mean, maybe there will be new elements, perhaps of ownership."

Manot went to Sylvia Beach and Penny Darnell, who were talking. Penny stepped away. "Mademoiselle Beach," he said, "you know we are here to try to restore recollections of the night of the party. What can you add to that?"

She shook her head. "Nothing. I was outside of

the group, really. I wanted to learn more about the book business."

Ricardo Camilo stood in a far corner with a wineglass in his hand. "You keep to yourself," Manot said.

"Yes, Inspector," Camilo answered. "I find that is best. I did the same on the night of the party. I speak most naturally in Spanish. The conversations were in English."

"Some say you appeared very angry that night. Was that with Mr. Thorndyke?"

Camilo said, "No. Martin Prince turned down my book that day. I was still upset. I was not in a talking mood. I've accepted that rejection now. When your investigation ends, I return to Spain."

Manot turned toward David Fitch, standing alone against a wall, arms folded across his chest. When Manot reached him, Fitch blurted out, "When does this charade end? What do you expect? Someone to confess to the killings?"

"Perhaps you, m'sieur, have something more to confess. About the death of the Detective Ward."

"I've told you everything. I didn't fight with him. I'm sure you've found no evidence of that, or you wouldn't be asking questions, going through all this. You'd be accusing me."

"The view of all is that at the first party, you gave your attentions freely to all the women here. Miss Minter . . ."

Fitch scowled but lowered his voice. "As you know now, I have a—a relationship—with Miss August."

"Yes."

"I did not want that to be obvious at the party, so

I pretended to take an interest in the beautiful young Miss Minter."

"A little show, for your wife?"

"Yes. And it worked, until that damned Ward intruded with his bloody camera. He got what he deserved."

Manot said, "I will note your comment in my file. That investigation is not yet over."

Seeing Patricia August watching him question Fitch, Manot proceeded to the spot where she sat. As he approached, she rose and said, "My turn at last? You seem to be enjoying your conversations."

"It is a duty."

"Then ask your questions, and be done with it."

"Just one that comes to mind. Did Mr. Prince discuss with you any special project he was working on with Eric Thorndyke?"

"He referred to a far-fetched idea. A movie script for talking pictures. *Talking*, you understand. Pictures don't talk."

"Did Martin Prince have that script? And did you see it?"

"No to both. At least, I didn't see it. Martin told me about it but dismissed it. I don't think he read it."

Manot walked toward Edda Van Eych. He checked his watch—nine-forty. Darnell would be sending word soon.

"Miss Van Eych." He smiled and nodded at her.

"I don't know how I can add to your inquiries."

"Just quickly—the night of the party, I believe you overheard discussions between Eric Thorndyke and Cynthia Fitch."

"I heard about his special project. A book, I thought. I tried to get more information about it, but

he said little more except to complain that Prince
turned him down. No surprise. He had turned me
down, and also Ricardo—Mr. Camilo." She paused.
"Then I discovered the project involved a film
script." She sniffed. "I had no interest in that."

"But someone did, Miss Van Eych. And enough,
perhaps, to kill for it."

Chapter Twenty-one

Monday night, December 30

Inspector Manot and Philip Thorndyke stood talking near the door to the bedroom in which Eric Thorndyke had been killed.

Manot said, "We've heard at least two versions of what happened that night. You said they heard you call out, one guest said the door was closed, later you said you might have closed it."

"I'm sorry if it has confused you. My father and I both took too much to drink that night. I realized later I may have closed the door when I went in. As I stand here now, in the same room, that's the best I can do."

A knock came at the main door to the suite, and an officer stationed at the door opened it to Darnell, Bardon, and the other two officers. Darnell strode over to Manot, Bardon following, and said, "Dead end."

Inspector Manot's face fell. "After all this."

"It happens. You know that. But we've determined one thing. The script is not in the rooms of any of these people."

Manot grimaced. "I do not like the words 'dead

end.' " He looked around the room. "Time to let these people go."

"Yes. We need to take one last look at our options and most-likely scenarios. And I have one more idea we can pursue. I don't know why I didn't think of it earlier."

"Tell me."

"When the suite is clear. Send them back to their rooms."

By eleven-thirty p.m., the once noisy suite was quiet. Bardon had returned to his office and all the party guests to their rooms. Darnell told Penny he'd be along in a while. Manot assigned one officer to search Prince's suite, and sent the others back to the station. He and Darnell took seats at a table in the deserted dining room.

"All right, John. Options, you say, and one more idea. We can use both."

"The script," Darnell said, pausing, "it connects the murders and the mystery. Let's summarize where we stand as simply as possible. Eric wrote it. It had value. It was in his room. After he was murdered, his son gave Eric's clothes to Adrian—he didn't admit that, but we know it's true—and Adrian paraded about as a ghost, in Philip's fuzzy thinking, to scare the killer into some kind of confession."

"An emotional, impractical approach," Manot said.

"Yes. Meanwhile the script disappears. Edda Van Eych asks about it but loses interest when she finds it's a script not a book. Then Charlotte Shelby asks about it, wants it pretty badly for her daughter."

"And others knew of the script."

"Yes. Philip, of course. The actress knew, hearing

it from Thorndyke. Prince knew of it, but may not have read it. Patricia August knew about it, but also may not have known much about it. The Fitches may have known something, but neither has indicated that."

"So where does that leave us?"

"With the people who knew something about what was in the script and what it's value was: Philip Thorndyke, Edda Van Eych, Patricia August, Charlotte Shelby, and the young actress. I think we can rule her out as to this kind of murder, but not in stealing the script."

"*Précisément*. There are two distinct types of crimes here."

"But I was coming to this—there's one other suspect we haven't considered, and I think now he's the most obvious one. Adrian."

"For the murders?"

"At least for stealing the script. Let's consider his type. He's willing to dress up in a dead man's clothes for money. He would have no qualms about stealing the script."

"How would he get access to it?"

"I knew you'd ask that, and I've just thought of the answer. When Philip gave him the clothing, he could have admitted Adrian to his father's bedroom. Maybe it was the first night the ghost appeared. He said, take what you need. And, left alone, he not only took the clothing, he saw the script and took it. An opportunist."

"Later he reads it and sees its value."

"Yes."

"But why kill Thorndyke, if he did, and why Prince?"

"I don't think he did kill them."

Manot's officer reported back to him, "Nothing, Inspector. I searched carefully."

"All right." Manot stood. "So we confront Adrian. He may have all the answers we need."

A pounding on the hall door disrupted their conversation, and Darnell watched as the officer opened it. A wide-eyed maid, one of the two he and Manot had interviewed, stood staring into the room.

"Inspector Manot—I am glad you are here." The woman rushed across the room to the Inspector. "A man is dead, Inspector! The magician. In his dressing room. Come quickly."

Inspector Manot bent over Adrian's body. "Dead," Manot said. "Stabbed in the back this time." He looked about the room watching the officer he had brought up with him search for a weapon. Philip Thorndyke sat on a chair at the far end of the small room.

Manot approached him. "You found the body? Tell us in detail what happened, please."

Thorndyke breathed in, looked up at Manot and Darnell. "I had an appointment with Adrian. He was to come to my room following his last show, after eleven. He didn't come. I came up to see if he was in his dressing room, and he was—just as you see him. I checked for a pulse, that's all." He looked at his hands and the white handkerchief he held in them, red with blood. "I got blood on my hands. I heard one of the maids in the hall, and ran out, told her to get you."

"You saw no one here?"

"No one."

"Did you disturb anything? Move or take anything?"

"You mean like a knife? No, nothing."

"And why were you going to see him tonight?"

"It was, well, personal."

Manot scowled. "There is nothing personal when we have a murder, m'sieur. You can tell me here, or at the *Sûreté*."

Thorndyke looked at Darnell, as if for help or advice, then back at Manot. "You probably guessed it anyway. He was the one I paid to act as my father's ghost. Three hundred pounds. I gave him the red cummerbund and bow tie my father had worn, to help create the illusion. I thought . . . I don't know . . . that the ghost image might unnerve the killer and reveal who it was. Then I gave him another three hundred."

Darnell asked, "And why were you here tonight?"

"He said he had something of value he would sell me."

"The script," Darnell said.

"How did you know?"

"You were going to buy it—buy it back?"

"He said there was no proof my father wrote it, and he'd sell it to me, that it had a lot of value." He took out a roll of bills. "This is what I had for him."

Manot nodded. "So he is dead and your money is saved. M'sieur, you must realize you are a suspect in this death, even though you have a very pretty story to tell. The maid has seen you with blood on your hands. You alone are found with the body. The rest of the tenth floor is deserted."

Thorndyke said in a dull voice, "I didn't do it.

You have to believe me on that. I had no reason to kill him."

Manot nodded to an officer, who came over to him. He asked him a question in French.

The officer shook his head, said something in French.

To Thorndyke, Manot said, "Do not attempt to leave the room. We will talk more." He and Darnell walked to the other side of the room. Manot said, "The officer found no knife. Looked everywhere."

"This is a different method of killing. Do you think it could be a different murderer?"

"I think it is the same one, using a different method," Manot said, "a convenient method. It could be Thorndyke."

"I don't see a motive there. He brought money with him, prepared to deal. You've called out the medical examiner."

"Yes."

"While we're waiting, let's search for the manuscript. It could be here. With this crime, you have a right to search."

They began searching desks, files, storage cabinets, dressing-table drawers, looking for some kind of bundle, not knowing exactly what it would look like, but challenging every suspicious-looking file and the contents of every receptacle.

"Nothing here," Darnell said, after a half hour's diligent search. "But there's one other place. His room, next to the showroom."

Leaving the officer with Thorndyke, Manot took Adrian's room key from the man's pocket and the two went to the magician's room. After another half hour's search, Darnell let out a whoop as he found the bundle in between layers of clothing in a closet. "This is it."

Manot stepped over and looked at it. "Not very imposing. Merely a sheaf of papers."

"That's all a script is. Paper. But it's the words on the paper that make it valuable." He opened a smaller envelope attached to the bundle. "Money here." He counted six bills. "Six hundred pounds." He handed it to Manot.

"I'm going to take Philip Thorndyke in and hold him on suspicion of murder, ask him some more questions. One night in jail may loosen his tongue. You've read Eric Thorndyke's notes. Take the script and read it tonight. I want to have your opinion in the morning. But for God's sake, don't lose it!"

Chapter Twenty-two

Tuesday morning, December 31

After a fitful night of little rest, staying up to read through the entire script, John Darnell rose early and went down for coffee while Penny still slept. Upon returning, he found Penny stirring in bed, and they ordered breakfast sent up to the room. After eating, he told her about Adrian's death, finding the script, and Philip's arrest.

Penny dressed for an outing. "Do you think the case is over now?"

"I don't think Philip killed Adrian, or anyone. The script is still the source of the motivations. Have to think about that."

"It's New Year's Eve, John. A good time to tell you some news."

Darnell nodded absently. "News? What kind of news?"

"Well, look at me, and I'll tell you."

John Darnell turned toward his wife. When she acted mysterious like this, he knew it was something important. He yanked his mind away from the case and focused on her. Her face seemed to have a special glow this morning. *News?* "All right," he said, "I'm ready."

"You know I've complained of feeling a bit queasy. No wine. Drinking only tea."

"The French diet is too rich for you."

"More than that, John. I—I've been holding something back from you, something I should have told you in London before we left there."

"You're ill?" He wondered at the anomaly of that thought. She looked as if she had the glow of life in her. A thought flashed in his mind. "We're going to have a baby?"

"Yes, John. Our first child."

He took her in his arms, gently, and kissed her. "That *is* news, wonderful news. I wouldn't have suspected . . ."

"I'm sorry I held back. I wanted to come to Paris. And I thought I'd tell you as soon as we returned to London. But, well, things took longer than I thought, and I was afraid my condition might become more noticeable. So there it is."

"I'm thrilled. I'm glad you told me now. We can talk about it on the long trip back home. We'll be leaving soon, I'm sure."

They talked more, making plans. Finally, Darnell looked at his watch. "Time to get going into the day. Things to do. And you? You'll want to be careful."

"Oh, John. I'm fine. In fact, I want to get out today, get some fresh air, some last looks, maybe, at Paris, if we're going to leave soon. Maybe Sylvia . . ."

"Okay, good. Let's get dressed. I'll have to see Manot, I know that much."

After Darnell dressed and left for a meeting with Inspector Manot, Penny suddenly felt at loose ends. She sat at the table in her dressing gown finishing the last of the orange juice, and thought about the day ahead. She stood looking out of their windows at the panorama of Paris in the bright sunlight. What to do in the next hours while John was busy? She had thought of some sort of expedition, such as more of the Louvre, and wondered if Sylvia Beach would be interested in another tour of it. She called the number Sylvia had given her at her apartment, but received no answer.

She poked about the room, and noticed the bundle on John's nightstand, looking like something to read. Was it the mysterious script they kept talking about? She glanced at the first page. Yes, a script. She took it to a chair by the window and sat with it in her lap. She'd read it, no harm done, and then call Sylvia again. Maybe she'd be home by then. She looked at the title on page one, *A Woman's Choice*, and began reading. The words flowed easily, and she soon became engrossed in the story. She nibbled at the remaining toast from breakfast, and finished the orange juice. And read on. In an hour, she had read about half of it, and was intrigued by the dark story line. The knock at her door interrupted her reading.

She opened the door to Cynthia Fitch, well dressed, as if ready to go out into the city.

"Hello," Cynthia said. "Your husband left word that he wanted to see me. I thought I'd stop by."

"John isn't here, but come in. I'm bored stiff today. I'm just doing some reading."

Cynthia looked at the two stacks of pages on the table near the window. "What is it?" Her face reflected her curiosity, her forehead furrowed and her eyes wide. She walked to the table, picked up a page, and read a few words. "A script."

"I wanted to finish it before John returned."

Cynthia's attitude changed. "I have a wonderful idea. I have some reading to do, too, in my purse. Bring it along; we'll have an outing and do our reading outdoors."

"Outing? Where?"

"How about La Tour Eiffel? To the top of the Eiffel Tower, and see Paris the way it should be seen. It's such a clear day. Some others are coming."

Penny hesitated, but at last said, "Wonderful. Have a seat. I'll just be a minute or two." She went into the bedroom, closed the door, quickly pulled on a dress, and selected a heavy outer jacket. She jotted a note and placed it on the bed. She took a quick glance in the mirror and stepped back into the living room.

"I'm ready. But we'll have to be back in two hours or so." She bundled up the script under her arm.

They took the elevator down to the main floor, chatting about the city and the tower. They walked to the front exit and the taxi stand. Penny asked, "Where are the others?"

Cynthia said, "I was to meet them there in half an hour. We'll have lunch together."

The doorman held open the taxi door for them as they jumped into the backseat. The driver turned around and gave a gap-toothed smile at the women. He said, *"Oui?"*

Cynthia Fitch said, "La Tour Eiffel," sat back, and, as the doorman closed the taxi door, smiled at Penny.

Cynthia Fitch fell silent, her mood black, as the taxi rattled through the streets toward the distant tower. Penny Darnell seemed absorbed in gazing out the window at the shops, hotels, and people as they moved along, and required no conversation. Cynthia took a deep breath, seeking relaxation of mind as well as body. The events of the past two weeks caved in upon her. Eric Thorndyke's murder. The investigation. Discovering—more like verifying—that her husband was having a very obvious affair with Patricia August. *The bitch!* She felt her hands tremble and clenched them together, as she did her teeth. She tried to hold herself together. She must do that.

"We're coming up to it," Penny exclaimed as they rounded a turn and rolled up the street to the broad walkway leading to the tower. They stepped out, and Cynthia gave the driver some coins.

Penny said, "It's magnificent!"

Cynthia forced herself back to the role of bright companion, and smiled, letting out her breath. "Let's buy our tickets."

At the ticket window, Cynthia bought two elevator tickets and they stood in the short line, only two people ahead of them, waiting for the elevator to return to the street level. They heard the rumbling and watched it as it slowly ratcheted its way down to them. At the street level, three passengers exited and the young man and woman in front of them entered the elevator. Cynthia took Penny's arm, and the two followed them inside.

Penny said, "I wonder where the others are."

"They're coming together. I expect they'll be here soon." Cynthia looked up as the elevator started to move, saying, "We're in for a treat."

As the elevator began its ascent, Penny said, "It's going up at an angle. I never thought—"

"Ingenious, isn't it? I'll never forget the first time I took this trip. Enjoy it, Penny. It may be a once in a lifetime experience."

"But you came back."

"Yes." She frowned. "From a different life."

Cynthia said nothing further as Penny, quiet now, looked down at the ground as the ride slanted up inside the tower. The unusual sense of direction disturbed all the passengers, and Cynthia even found herself taking the rail for balance, as Penny and the other two did. The white-haired operator of the elevator smiled and held his hand steady on the control, looking up and ahead of the car into the superstructure of the tower.

The car eased to a stop, and the elevator doors clanged open at the touch of the operator. The two young people left the car quickly and walked arm in arm to the far corner of the open observation deck and looked out at the city. The boy put his arm around the girl, and their two silhouettes became one.

Cynthia walked to the railing across from the elevator, feeling the presence of Penny beside her, but not looking at her. As they reached the rail, they both gazed out upon the houses, churches, buildings, streets, vehicles, and people hundreds of feet below them, everything seeming smaller, almost miniaturized. Cynthia recalled the first time she had viewed the scene. A happier time, then, before forces beyond her control had torn her apart from her secure life.

Penny said, "You were right. This is a great place to take a last look at Paris."

Cynthia glanced sidelong at her. "Yes, a last look." At the far end of the rail, she watched the two young people, not yet eighteen, she guessed, embracing. Her black mood returned, even deeper this time, but she knew she must keep her strength up and steady for what she was to do.

After some minutes, as the elevator returned to the observation deck after a trip down, the two young people walked over to the door, which opened. One person stepped out on the platform, a gray-haired, heavy man, walking with a limp. The boy and girl entered and the elevator began to descend. The man walked to the rail, some distance from Cynthia and Penny.

Cynthia breathed in the clean air, freshened by breezes at that height. She stood close to Penny, noticing her, but looking straight ahead at the sweeping view.

"I could stay up here forever," Penny said. "But I do wish the others would arrive." She looked around the platform. Somewhere below, a distant bell tolled. One o'clock.

Cynthia said nothing, deep into her own thoughts. Minutes passed and the elevator once again returned to the platform. No one exited, but the older man limped aboard the car, and it began its slow descent. Cynthia and Penny were alone on the platform.

Inspector Manot and his officers crossed the lobby quickly, heading toward Darnell, who had just come from the bank of elevators. "Let's compare notes," Darnell said, as soon as he reached him. They took seats in a corner of the lobby.

"Did you learn anything from Philip Thorndyke?"

Manot said, "No, and we can only hold him until tonight."

"Unless you charge him?"

"Yes. Now tell me about the script."

"I think it holds the answer to the question of who the killer might be and why the killings have occurred."

"That sounds a little too vague."

"I'll tell you about it. Then you decide. Here's a script set in London, in modern times. Could be today, last year. It's a triangle among two men and a woman. The woman is married to one of the men, and in love, having a torrid affair, with the other."

"Sounds familiar. Like Paris."

"Or any other city. But this is in London, where Eric Thorndyke lived. Listen to the names of the characters—Rick Thornwall, Cindy Finch, Daniel Finch. Do they sound familiar?"

"I don't understand."

"Compare them—Eric Thorndyke, Rick Thornwall . . . Cynthia Fitch, Cindy Finch . . . David Fitch, Daniel Finch."

"He put the three of them into the script?"

"Exactly. With descriptions to match and details of their affair. That's the love triangle—Eric, Cynthia, and David. And that's our motive, but we're not sure who acted upon it."

"What do you think?"

"Eric's story would be damaging to Cynthia and David. It could go either way. Either one could have tried to bury the script by silencing the author."

"It seems to let out Charlotte Shelby. She wouldn't care if the script came out. The publicity might even help a movie."

"Right. Same for Prince, if he read it. It narrows down to Cynthia and David Fitch."

"Then we go up now."

At the Fitches' room, Darnell and Manot found the husband alone. "We need to talk with you and Mrs. Fitch," Manot said.

David looked at them with a blank expression. "Cynthia isn't here. In fact, I don't know where she is.

I was, well, talking with Miss August, and just returned. It looks like Cynthia's gone out for a while."

"Gone out where?"

"I really don't know."

Darnell said, "We know what's in the script, David."

"Script? What are you talking about?"

"Thorndyke's script."

Fitch shook his head. "You're not making any sense to me. Maybe you need to talk to Cynthia. She talked with Thorndyke."

"At the first party?"

"Yes. When else?"

Darnell frowned. "We've got to find her. Maybe someone in the lobby knows something. But I want to stop by my room first."

Manot nodded. "I'll go on down to the lobby. Five minutes from now. Meet me at the desk."

Darnell hurried to his room, while Manot strode down to the elevators. Inside their room, Darnell called out, "Penny?" He walked rapidly through the rooms. In the bedroom he saw the note on the bed:

*John, dear—Taking last look at Paris with Cynthia
Fitch and some other women. Back in two or
three hours.*

Darnell's heart jumped into his throat at the words. He rushed to the closet, opened a suitcase, and took out his .38 special, checked it, and dropped it his pocket. He ran to the elevators and at the lobby level ran out looking for Manot. He found him at the desk with two of his officers. He blurted out, "Cynthia Fitch has taken Penny with her somewhere!"

Manot's eyes widened. *"Mon Dieu!"* He gestured

at the desk clerk. "M'sieur Alain said he saw the two of them cross the lobby toward the front exit half an hour ago."

Darnell strode rapidly toward the Champs-Elysses exit. He saw Hemingway sitting near the door and asked him, breathlessly, "Did you happen to see my wife leave the hotel?"

Hemingway said, "Yes, I did, Professor. I was just taking this seat when they walked by me."

"They?"

"Your wife and the millionaire's wife, Cynthia." He looked into the Professor's anxious eyes. "If it's important—well, I did hear a bit of their conversation."

"Please! Quickly!"

"It wasn't much. Just the word 'tower.' Something about seeing the tower."

Darnell ran out the front door and grabbed the doorman by his lapels. "Did you see two women come out, going to the tower, about half an hour ago?"

The startled doorman looked from the Inspector to Darnell and said, "*Oui, m'sieur*. They take a taxi. To La Tour Eiffel."

Manot ordered his officer to bring their car up from where it was parked half a block away. In minutes, he, Darnell, and the two officers had all piled into the car. As the engine started, Hemingway pulled open the door and said, "I'm going, too," and jumped into the front seat next to the officer who was driving. The car roared away.

Cynthia Fitch knew what must be done. She had spent a sleepless night in doubt, but seeing Penny with the script crystalized everything in her tormented mind. She looked around the platform once more. Yes, deserted. No one but herself and Penny Darnell. *Darnell!* The very name made the bile rise in her throat. *He ruined everything, and he'll pay for it!*

As she stared at the city below, thoughts swirled and memories flashed through Cynthia's angry mind. Memories of the vicious words Eric Thorndyke said to her at the party two weeks ago . . . his threats to tell her husband of their dying affair, to give Fitch the script, which laid out the affair in detail, even with locations her husband knew of, nothing left to the imagination, and no question as to who the characters were. Thorndyke hinted that he'd already offered it for sale to Prince, and that Prince might have read it. He knew it would ruin her plans to divorce David for a multimillion-pound settlement. *How could I have ever loved such a man? Or trusted him?*

Then the memories of the night she confronted Martin Prince rushed into her thoughts, along with his harsh, unfeeling words when he told her that a drunken Thorndyke had confided in him about their affair. How he'd shown her the note from Adrian, the same one she'd received, and how Prince decided to join with Fitch in taking over American-Universal, on condition that Prince would become President. He'd revealed her affair with Thorndyke to David Fitch to gain leverage and use the script in a future picture. How she pleaded with Prince not to do it, and how he had laughed at her, turned his back on her, and then how she . . .

And memories of the final scene with the damned magician who revealed he had the script and was trying to blackmail her. The tenth floor had been deserted then, like a tomb, the dressing room she slipped into where she waited until the magician came in after the show, empty. How she asked to see the script when he came in at exactly eleven, and how he laughed at her, revealing a cruel streak his audiences never suspected beneath the pleasant banter and smiles. *"The money first. Five thousand pounds. It's gone up. But a cheap price to avoid jail."*

Her words, *"Love is no crime."*

"Murder is. Do you have the money?"

She remembered saying, *"This is obscene."* And her realization of what she must do. *"Prove to me you have it."*

Adrian had shrugged his shoulders and handed her a single sheet with a nonchalant air, and turned his back. She watched him close his eyes as he spread cleansing cream over his face, and saw her chance. She remembered how she fingered the garotte in her purse for a second, saw the sharp letter-knife on his table, grabbed it up and stabbed him in the back, viciously, and again . . . and again.

Cynthia's hands jerked abruptly on the rail, and Penny turned toward her. "What is it? The height?"

"No. It's nothing. Go on and enjoy the view." But her breath was coming in gasps now. She felt she couldn't breathe.

Penny turned back to take a last look. "I've seen enough."

"Yes, you have," Cynthia said, her lips tight and her eyes wild now. She pulled a tough leather cord from her pocket and twisted it about Penny's neck, turning it, making it tighter. Penny gasped and choked, her arms flailed, and her hands tried to pull the cord away from her throat. She kicked out with her heels, backward, as Cynthia Fitch's eyes blazed with a fury that embodied all the frustrations and guilt of the past two weeks. Her strength and obsession only increased.

The damned professor! He may have even read the script! But this will stop him. Her thoughts raged as Penny Darnell slumped in her grip, closer now to the platform floor. Neither of them heard the elevator arrive or the door clang open, or the running footsteps of the men who charged across the platform.

John Darnell instinctively struck Cynthia Fitch on the back of her neck with the weapon in his hand, his drawn gun. The woman stumbled, released her grip on the leather thong, which then fell from Penny's throat.

Darnell caught Penny before she hit the floor as she fell away from Cynthia's grip. He put his gun away and cradled her in his arms. "Penny! Are you all right?"

Cynthia Fitch staggered toward the railing, the script falling to the floor of the viewing platform. "I'll jump," Cynthia said, with wild eyes, as she tried to scale the railing. But Inspector Manot reached her in time and grasped her around the waist, throwing her to the floor. An officer knelt down with handcuffs and put them on the woman's hands, behind her back, and secured manacles on her legs.

Freed from the strangling cord, Penny coughed and took in a sharp breath. She managed to say, in a raw voice, "John . . . Thank God . . ."

In the confusion, Hemingway gathered up the script from the floor where the wind had started to separate the pages. He took it over to the elevator area, out of the wind, and began reading it, skimming the pages rapidly, realizing the significance of the names. He gleamed as much from it as he could, knowing he'd have to surrender it to the police soon.

"Don't try to talk," John said to Penny. "It's all right, now—it's all right, dear."

Manot motioned with a thumb to his two officers. "Take the prisoner into the elevator," Manot said, "and down to the car. Get a cab. Then send the elevator back for us."

They took Cynthia Fitch down and secured her in the car, one officer remaining with her, the other hiring a cab, ordering it to wait there, and returning in the elevator for the others. When all were below, Manot and the officers left for the station, while Darnell, Penny, and Hemingway returned to the hotel in the cab.

In the cab, Darnell held Penny close to him, his eyes moist with emotion, saying, "It's over now. You're safe. We're all safe, now."

Penny nodded, and spoke, as if only to prove that she could use her voice. "Someday, John . . . someday, tell me why this all happened . . . but not now. Not right now."

Chapter Twenty-three

Tuesday evening, December 31

Darnell took Penny back to their rooms and called Bardon, who brought Dr. Pascal up to inspect and treat Penny immediately. "The neck looks worse than it is," the doctor said. "It was caught in time. Now, this ointment will help. In a week, it will be almost back to normal."

Inspector Manot called from *Sûreté* headquarters to say that Cynthia Fitch had been officially placed under arrest for the murders of Eric Thorndyke, Martin Prince, and Adrian, and for the attempted murder of Penny Darnell.

Two hours later Manot knocked on Darnell's door and they sat together in the living room. Darnell poured sherry for the two of them, as Penny lay in bed, resting.

"Madame Fitch confessed, John," Manot said, "after we took her in. I did not have to ask her. She seemed to want to tell it all, once we had her. Guilt, I suppose. The realization that it was all over finally. She admitted all three murders."

"All for money, of course."

Manot's voice took on an ironic tinge. "Yes. She wanted a divorce from David Fitch, and half of his millions. She knew he was having an affair. But under English law, she would not only have to have a pure record herself, but also evidence of his infidelity, in order to claim half his wealth. But she had been having an affair with Thorndyke, who was going to tell Fitch in the form of the script. He had already let Martin Prince know of it, and Prince was also about to tell Fitch, to save him millions of pounds in divorce money and gain favor in American-Universal's acquisition, when he heard Fitch planned the takeover. She could have lost everything if either Eric or Prince talked. They both had to die."

"They were going to blow the whistle," Darnell said.

"What?"

"Tell the world about the affair."

"Yes." Manot went on. "Thorndyke was unfaithful to her and finally rejected her. When he was drunk, he'd talk about her. Wrote the damaging script. She *had* to kill him, in her words, and Prince. She killed Adrian in a rage to silence him."

"After one murder, the second becomes easier."

"*Oui*. And the scorned woman was emotionally disturbed." Manot screwed up a crooked smile. "One odd footnote—"

"Yes?"

"David Fitch came to headquarters when he heard of her arrest and visited her in her cell. He told her he'd be getting her the best Paris and London lawyers he could to take up her case." Manot ran a hand through his tangled hair. "But the woman said nothing. Since her confession, John, she has not said one single word."

* * *

Later, Penny looked up at her husband, who bent over her to examine her wound as she lay in bed. "I'm feeling better, now."

"Would you like a sherry?"

She shook her head. "Just water. My throat's dry." Penny took a deep breath. "I was so shocked, John, when I felt the cord around my neck from behind. I knew it had to be Cynthia, because no one else was up there. But I couldn't believe it. I couldn't breathe, I couldn't scream, and I just could not get that cord from around my throat. It seemed to get deeper and deeper as I struggled."

"Please—you don't have to relive it, Penny."

"Things were growing dim when you arrived."

"Thank God we were in time. If she had succeeded . . . Two lives were at stake."

"I know. But we're all safe, now. And ready to go home. You can start packing our bags. But right now, I'm sleepy. I'm wanting a little nap, John."

He nodded, kissed her on the forehead, pulled the door closed, and stepped into the living room.

An hour later, as he was gathering clothes together for the suitcase, someone rapped lightly on the door. When he opened it, he saw it was Philip Thorndyke.

Thorndyke said, "Thank you, Professor. I promised you a fee for your part in this, and a check will be delivered to your room by my bank today. I'm sorry your wife was endangered." He held up the script that was bundled under an arm. "I will sell this. I have one person interested in it already—Charlotte Shelby. She wants it for a movie for her daughter."

Darnell picked up a slim journal from a table.

"And here's your father's notebook about the script. It may help."

Thorndyke took it. "I'll read it on the way back to America. And the script. These are the last things my father worked on, things that he believed in. They were important to him, and I'll try hard to make something of them—for his sake."

"Any regrets?"

"We never should have come on this trip. And, of course, my big mistake was hiring Adrian to act as my father's ghost. I thought it would bring the killer out into the open, but it led to Adrian's death."

Darnell said, "No, Philip. You didn't cause that. That was greed, twisted into theft and blackmail, and it fostered his own murder. He made his death likely. Cynthia Fitch made it fact."

By that evening, New Year's Eve, news of the arrest of Cynthia Fitch and the conclusion of the case spread rapidly among the hotel guests who had come to Paris at Martin Prince's invitation. *Directeur* Jacques Bardon announced he would arrange a celebratory dinner that evening for all of them, at the hotel's expense. And it was a lavish affair, allowing them to relax and say their good-byes. Penny insisted on attending, wearing a high-neck jacket and scarf to conceal her wound. The food and wine, all agreed, were excellent, and the view on the clear night from the large table by the window overlooking the Champs-Elysees, with the Eiffel Tower in the distance, was overwhelming.

Gazing out upon the vista, Penny said, "This is

something I'll always remember, John. Our last, wonderful dinner in Paris."

After the meal, Bardon presented Penny with a small package. "For you," he said, "to remember Paris."

Penny took it with some trepidation, thinking her private news may have been revealed. She opened the package, as John Darnell and the others watched, and removed its contents—a gray metal, eight-inch tall, perfect replica of the Eiffel Tower. She shook her head. "I don't need this to help me remember."

Later in their room, as they packed, Darnell said, "I've been thinking about redoing some things in our flat. That small room upstairs across the hall we use for your sewing, and odds and ends . . . ?"

"I know what you're thinking, John. It would be a perfect nursery."

"Sung and I will get it ready."

Penny laughed. "No rush. We have about eight months to go. I think it'll be in August. I talked with Dr. Pascal."

"I called the train station. We leave tomorrow morning. I want to get you home."

She put her arms around him. "And I want to go home, John." She rested a hand on her stomach. "We all want to go home."

The next day, New Year's Day, as the taxi driver drove them through the crowded streets of the city, John and Penny Darnell took a last look at Paris, drinking in the sights and sounds of the city of light, where so much had transpired over the past two weeks, where danger had touched their lives, and where realization had begun of the bright change in their future that would become more and more apparent in the months ahead.

Seeing the Eiffel Tower in the distance, John nodded at the package on the seat beside him. "We have your souvenir of that—an ironic gift—to put on the mantel at home."

Penny linked her arm in his. "I'll leave the one unpleasant memory behind, and take home to London the good ones, like my time with Sylvia, seeing the Louvre, meeting your brave soldier, and seeing how young love developed between him and the beautiful movie star. But one day I hope we'll return to Paris to enjoy La Tour Eiffel properly. Now . . . well, we return to a new life not only for us but also for another little Darnell."

Darnell mused. "If it's a boy . . ."

Penny smiled at him. "You know something, John? I think we *will* have a boy. I just have that feeling."

He went on thoughtfully, "We might include Jeffrey in his name in some way. After my brother, you know?"

She nodded. "That would be wonderful."

Penny Darnell looked out the window, silent now, holding her husband's arm, feeling secure with him next to her, and dreaming ahead, with all the peace and comfort of a new mother-to-be. Penny didn't know quite how, yet, to communicate to her husband her exciting, inchoate feelings of expectation. But she wanted to share everything with him over these coming months—her wonder and awe at the thought of becoming a mother, all the new and personal and complex feelings that came with it.

Penny shivered suddenly, and knew it was not from the cold. And then she realized that John, too,

Sam McCarver

would be jolted out of his comfortable pattern of existence. So they would help each other to work through and enjoy every minute of this incredible change in their lives. She breathed a deep sigh of contentment, looked at her husband, and squeezed his arm. And John Darnell smiled, as if he already knew exactly what was in her heart.

Epilogue

The guests of Martin Prince—who had come to know each other more intimately than they ever expected during their two-week enforced stay at the hotel—said their good-byes and took their departures on New Year's Day. Their paths led in different directions, but with some intersections.

David Fitch hired the best English and French attorneys for Cynthia. Her trial resulted in her indeterminate confinement in a mental institution for treatment, pending later imprisonment. She had spoken no words at all since being taken into custody. Fitch placed a significant sum in trust in France, for Cynthia's lifetime care. He acquired a controlling interest in American-Universal Publishing, secured a divorce, and moved to New York. A year later, he and Trisha married in a quiet ceremony and traveled by train from New York to Monterey, California, taking a room there in a luxury hotel overlooking the Pacific Ocean.

Philip Thorndyke did not produce his father's script as a movie until 1929, but then only after changing the names, and without any of the three stars his father wanted for the female role.

Ricardo Camilo married Edda Van Eych, and the two of them built a life together in Barcelona. She finished rewriting her book, telling the dangerous real-life story of her father as a peacemaker in Germany before the war, and the experiences that led to his death, as a nonfiction work. She sold it to another publisher.

Camilo rewrote his book with scenes realistically describing the uprising within Spain. Three years later his book was published and became a popular silent movie. And in 1936, his story turned into fact as the Spanish Civil War began. He was shot and wounded in one of the last battles, but survived.

John and Penny Darnell returned to their home in London, a base from which Darnell would continue to pursue his investigations of reported supernatural events and sightings in England, Europe, and the world as his international reputation widened. And during 1919, Penny prepared herself for a new and exciting life experience—the birth of her first child. Now that she would be bringing her first child into the world there, London at last truly felt, to Penny Darnell, like home.

Historical Note

And the "real people" in this book . . . ?

Sylvia Beach secured enough encouragement for her to set up her own bookstore, and she opened it with the proud name Shakespeare and Company. In 1922 she helped publish *Ulysses*, the first book written by James Joyce, and turned her shop into a meeting place for him and others in the world of literature.

Mary Miles Minter returned to Hollywood and made many popular silent pictures, some directed by the older, debonair William Desmond Taylor, with whom she had a love affair. In February 1922, Taylor was murdered. Mabel Normand, the actress, and Mary's mother, Charlotte, initially were suspects, but when police discovered Mary's nightgown with the initials *M.M.M.* in Taylor's home, she became the prime suspect. Not charged for lack of evidence, she still lost her movie career before reaching twenty due to the bad publicity.

Talking pictures did not succeed in any significant way for eight years after 1919. In 1921, *Dream Street* was released, with some fanfare, as the first full-length "talkie" movie made with an integrated soundtrack rather than loosely coordinated phonograph records. But in 1927, *The Jazz Singer*, featuring four songs by popular entertainer Al Jolson and a few conversations recorded in sound in the film, fascinated and delighted audiences across America, and ultimately across the world. Movies could talk, and scripts had at last become important.

Ernest Hemingway had the war experiences described in this book, but never revealed what really happened between Christmas and New Year's Eve, 1918. He claimed, slyly, that he spent the week in Sicily with a young woman. He took his ship from Genoa back to America—New York, then Chicago. After some years of finding himself and resolving, with serious intent, to become a writer, he married and returned to Paris in 1921. He met Sylvia Beach, who then had her store, and he was mentored by writer Gertrude Stein. He stalked Paris streets, consumed prodigious amounts of wine in its quaint bars, and published a book of short stories and poems in 1923.

He met F. Scott Fitzgerald in the Dingo Bar in Paris, and accepted Fitzgerald's editing of his first novel, *The Sun Also Rises*, published with success in 1926. In 1929 he wrote *A Farewell to Arms*, also mirroring broadly his World War I experiences—a wounded soldier, a nurse, and love. A war correspondent in the Spanish Civil War from 1936 to 1939, Hemingway engaged in battles in Spain, narrowly escaping with his life. His 1940 novel, *For Whom the Bell Tolls*, reflected his impressions of the war. And his 1952 novella, *The Old Man and the Sea*, earned Ernest Hemingway a Nobel Prize.

Sam McCarver
The John Darnell Mysteries

CASE OF CABIN 13   19690-2

The year is 1912. John Darnell is a professional investigator whose specialty is debunking theories of paranormal activities. A bizarre series of apparent suicides in cabin 13 on three different White Star Line ships has the Managing Director frantic. Darnell agrees to take passage on their newest ship, the *Titanic*, to investigate, and once on board, he suspects the reported suicides were really murders. But when the fate of the *Titanic* is sealed in the icy waters of the Atlantic, will the killer get away with yet another murder?

THE CASE OF COMPARTMENT 7   19959-6

Now the world's first and only "paranormal detective" climbs aboard the Orient Express--with a sultry spy, a phantom bride, and a budding mystery writer named Agatha Christie.

THE CASE OF THE 2ND SÉANCE   20160-4

During a séance, the daughter of England's Prime Minister vanishes. It's up to paranormal investigator John Darnell and famous author Sir Arthur Conan Doyle to find her.

THE CASE OF THE RIPPER'S REVENGE   20458-1

Detective John Darnell teams up with George Bernard Shaw to track down a murderer whose crimes bear a disturbing resemblance to Jack the Ripper's.

To order call: 1-800-788-6262

Hazel Holt

"Sheila Malory is a most appealing heroine."
—Booklist

MRS. MALORY AND THE DELAY OF EXECUTION
0-451-20627-4

When a schoolteacher at a prestigious English prep school dies suddenly, Mrs. Malory gets shanghaied into being substitute teacher.

MRS. MALORY AND THE FATAL LEGACY
0-451-20002-0

Sheila Malory returns, this time as executor to the estate of a late, bestselling novelist. And what Malory reads into the death is a crime.

MRS. MALORY AND THE LILIES THAT FESTER
0-451-20354-2

When the unsavory Mr. Masefield is murdered, locals and the law blame Sheila Malory's future daughter-in-law. Now Sheila must untangle the truth before the real killer strikes again.

To order call: 1-800-788-6262

Peter Tremayne
The Sister Fidelma Mysteries

Set in Ireland circa 600 A.D., the Sister Fidelma Mysteries
capture the spirit of a time long past, when throughout
Europe, Ireland was a by-word for literacy and learning,
and a place where women held equal sway. Sister Fidelma,
a young advocate in the ancient Irish courts, generally finds
herself called to untangle a complex web of murder too
often in the face of some all too swift, misguided justice.

Ingeniously plotted and subtly paced, these novels are
written with a feel for the times that provides them with a
refeshing authenticity. Once you meet this brilliant and
beguiling heroine you will not want to stop reading.

Absolution by Murder	**19299-0**
Shroud for the Archbishop	**19300-8**
Suffer Little Children	**19557-4**
The Subtle Serpent	**19558-2**
The Spider's Web	**19559-0**
Valley of the Shadow	**20330-5**

To order call: 1-800-788-6262